Out of the Dark

Out of the Dark

(Du plus loin de l'oubli)

PATRICK MODIANO

Translated by Jordan Stump

University of Nebraska Press

Lincoln

⊗ The paper in this
book meets the
minimum requirements
of American National
Standard for
Information Sciences –
Permanence of Paper
for Printed Library
Materials, ANSI Z
39.48-1984.
Library of Congress
Cataloging-in-
Publication Data
Modiano, Patrick, 1945–
[Du plus loin de l'oubli.
English] Out of the
dark = Du plus loin
de l'oubli / Patrick
Modiano ; translated by
Jordan Stump. p. cm.
ISBN 0-8032-3196-2
(hardcover : alk.
paper). – ISBN 0-
8032-8229-X (pbk. :
alk. paper) I. Stump,
Jordan, 1959–
II. Title.
PQ2673.03D8313 1998
843'.914—dc21
98-13100 CIP

Translator's Introduction

I find it difficult to preface this novel without alluding to a very different age – nearly thirty years before the publication of *Out of the Dark* in France – and to a year that looms large in the French imagination: 1968. This was a year of many changes in France. A massive springtime uprising among students and workers paralyzed the nation, shaking many of its most solidly established institutions (notably the university system) to their foundations and ushering in a newly visible and newly powerful youth culture, a culture of contestation and anti-traditionalism that would dramatically change the look and feel of the country. Charles de Gaulle, who had dominated French politics since the early days of World War II, would not survive the blow to his credibility and reputation dealt by his intransigence toward the young revolutionaries; he would resign early the following year. De Gaulle was not alone: many of the great icons of twentieth-century France were finding themselves forced to make way for something new. Jean-Paul Sartre was openly mocked by the insurgent students when he tried to join one of their rallies. The daring of the New Novelists, the avant-garde of the decade before, was beginning to seem less daring than the work of the so-called New New Novelists, who were blending a purely literary discourse with a new critical and theoretical awareness influenced by structuralism and semiotics. And the purely theoretical discourse of those disciplines – and most particularly of deconstruction and poststructuralism – was beginning to imprint itself on the public imagination, allowing a rigorous and implacable questioning of language, truth, and the ideologies behind them. Existentialism and humanism were rapidly losing ground to a far more radical way of thinking, whose influence is still with us today. In many ways, 1968 was a moment when the shape of the century changed.

It was also in 1968 that Éditions Gallimard published Patrick Modiano's first novel, *La Place de l'Étoile*, which brought its twenty-three-year-old author immediate critical and public acclaim. *La Place de l'Étoile* is not fully a product of its time: it is not exactly rebellious or transgressive in the way that many texts by young writers were at that time, and it does not incorporate the latest advances in structuralist or poststructuralist theory. Its gaze is turned not toward a bright revolutionary future but toward a rather faded past, and toward a subject that might have seemed strangely anachronistic to the forward-looking reader of the late sixties: the place of the Jew in France. The novel's protagonist, a presumably young man with the unlikely name of Raphael Schlemilovitch, haunts the holy places of Frenchness, from seaside resorts to Alpine meadows, contaminating them with his very presence, not unlike a character in a novel by the virulently anti-Semitic Céline, of whose writing *La Place de l'Étoile* provides a devastating pastiche. This harsh, funny, profoundly ironic novel offers no hopeful visions for the future; rather, dredging up old hostilities that France would prefer to forget, it casts the Jew as a continual outsider, a pariah, an object of acute terror and loathing. The nation's past, it would seem, could not be done away with quite so easily as some would wish.

Today *La Place de l'Étoile* seems as thoroughly singular a novel as ever, standing well apart from its contemporaries. Indeed, both in style and in subject, it is a deeply *personal* book, whose themes of persecution and exclusion have their roots in Modiano's own family background. His father was a Jew of Alexandrian extraction, his mother an aspiring actress from Belgium; the couple met and fell in love in the uneasy Paris of the early forties. Modiano was born in 1945, and his childhood was profoundly marked by memories of the Occupation, the Deportation, and the atmosphere of menace and clandestinity that had haunted the years just before his birth. Even if Modiano himself did not live through that dark time, he nevertheless 'remembers' it, both as a historical event and as a way of life, a free-floating and pervasive presence. It is this presence, this unfading past, that forms the backdrop for all his novels, obsessively returning, though never in the same form – only as a palpable but indefinable ambience whose source is never made clear, and that cannot simply be traced to one chronological moment. In other words, Modiano does not write 'historical' novels, even if they are all profoundly shaped by a certain history, a history of marginalization and effacement. Time and again, his central characters are caught up in an atmosphere of exclusion, imminent danger, uncertain or concealed identities; time and again they find themselves in milieux that are about to be wiped out by the approaching shadows: quaintly glamorous resorts, elegant clubs, places of innocent pleasure for movie stars or up-and-coming champions in tennis or skiing. The story is always the same, and yet the great preoccupation of Modiano's writing cannot be defined by one event, even if it is always a question of the same phenomenon: nothing less (and nothing more precise) than the obliteration of a past.

So insistently does this story recur that Modiano is often said to be 'forever writing the same book.' This is not exactly true: each novel has a perfectly distinct (if sometimes bewildering) plot, perfectly defined (if sometimes ambiguous) characters, a particular (if sometimes permeable) setting in time and space. Still, there is a very strong phenomenon of repetition at work in Modiano's writing, both within each novel and from one to another. It is not only the same tale of loss that repeats itself in his books; again and again, we find ourselves before the same colors (blue in particular), the same sounds (a voice half covered by some sort of noise), the same settings (empty rooms, deserted streets), even the same gestures (an arm raised in greeting or farewell, a forehead pressed against a windowpane). In themselves, these repetitions create a haunting and unforgettable atmosphere, instantly recognizable to any reader familiar with Modiano's work; set against the overwhelming sense of loss and disappearance that is the novels' other most visible element, they make of our reading a deeply disorienting experience, sad and strange. Everything disappears, his books seem to tell us, and also – in small but omnipresent echoes – everything somehow stays. This presence of an obliterated past is meant neither to comfort us nor to terrify us: it is there to remind us endlessly of that loss, I think, so that the loss is not itself lost, so that it remains sharp, insistent, present, so that we are continually called to a life that has long since disappeared.

This is the story told by *Out of the Dark,* Modiano's fourteenth novel, which appeared in 1996. Its setting is not the Occupation but the early sixties; nevertheless, the oppressive, menacing atmosphere of that earlier time seems to have lingered long after its disappearance. The young narrator, like his friends or even his older self, appears to be on the run from something (but what?), living a strangely worried life whose uncertain joys seem always about to be wiped out; like his friends or even his older self, he has a vaguely marginal air about him, even if we can't quite see why he should or what makes him so. We are far from the dark days of the past, then, but strangely close as well.

At the same time, however, *Out of the Dark* is a sadly funny and touching love story and a personal reminiscence that may well seem oddly familiar to many readers. This is perhaps the most extraordinary of Modiano's feats as a writer: however private his work seems, however inseparable from a personal past, it always speaks to us of something we feel we know, as if these were our own faded memories, our own shapeless uncertainties and apprehensions, our own loose ends. The potency of his strikingly simple, enigmatic, and profoundly moving prose is no secret in France, where Modiano is a perennial best-seller and a household name, still enjoying the same critical acclaim and public success that greeted his first novel. Outside of academic circles, however, most readers in the United States have yet to discover him; they have a great surprise in store.

*

Modiano is never easy to translate; the apparent simplicity and neutrality of his style conceals a wealth of subtle difficulties for the translator, and I wish to thank here several people who helped me through those difficulties. The French title of this book, *Du plus loin de l'oubli,* poses a particularly thorny problem, since the English language has no real equivalent for *oubli,* nor even a simple way of saying *du plus loin.* The phrase, taken from a French translation of a poem by the German writer Stefan George, is literally equivalent to 'from the furthest point of forgottenness,' and I have found no way to express this idea with the eloquent simplicity of the original. I would like to extend my most grateful thanks to Eleanor Hardin for coming up with the current title, and for all the invaluable help she has given me with this translation; thanks, too, to Warren Motte and Tom Vosteen for their sympathetic reading and insightful suggestions.

Out of the Dark

For Peter Handke

Du plus loin de l'oubli . . .
Stefan George

She was a woman of average height; he, Gérard Van
Bever, was slightly shorter. The night of our first meeting, that winter thirty years ago, I had gone with them
to a hotel on the Quai de la Tournelle and found myself
in their room. Two beds, one near the door, the other
beneath the window. The window didn't face the quai,
and as I remember it was set into a gable.

Nothing in the room was out of place. The beds were
made. No suitcases. No clothes. Only a large alarm clock,
sitting on one of the nightstands. And despite that alarm
clock, it seemed as though they were living here in secret,
trying to leave no sign of their presence. We had spent
only a brief moment in the room that first night, just long
enough to drop off some art books I was tired of carrying, which I hadn't managed to sell to a secondhand book
dealer on the Place Saint-Michel.

And it was on the Place Saint-Michel that they had first
spoken to me, late that afternoon, as all around us the
crowds streamed down the steps to the métro or up the
boulevard in the opposite direction. They had asked me
where they might find a post office nearby. I was afraid
my directions might be too vague for them to follow,
since I've never been able to describe the shortest route
between two points. I had decided it would be best to

5

show them to the Odéon post office myself. On the way there, she had stopped in a café-tabac and bought three stamps. As she stuck them to the envelope, I had time to read the address: Majorca.

She had slipped the letter into one of the mailboxes without checking to see whether it was the one marked AIR MAIL – FOREIGN. We had turned back toward the Place Saint-Michel and the quais. She was concerned to see me carrying the books, since 'they were probably heavy.' She had said sharply to Gérard Van Bever:

'You could help him.'

He had smiled at me and taken one of the books – the largest – under his arm.

In their room on the Quai de la Tournelle, I had set the books at the foot of the nightstand, the one with the alarm clock. I couldn't hear it ticking. The hands pointed to three o'clock. A spot on the pillowcase. Bending down to set the books on the floor, I had noticed a smell of ether coming from the pillow and the bed. Her arm had brushed against me, and she had switched on the bedside lamp.

We had dined in a café on the quai, next door to their hotel. We had ordered only the main dish of that night's special. Van Bever had paid the check. I had no money with me that night, and Van Bever thought he was five francs short. He had searched through the pockets of his overcoat and his jacket and finally found five francs in change. She said nothing and watched him absently, smoking a cigarette. She had given us her dish to share and had eaten only a few bites from Van Bever's plate.

6

She had turned to me and said in her slightly gravelly voice:

'Next time we'll go to a real restaurant. . . .'

Later, we had both waited by the front door of the hotel while Van Bever went up to the room for my books. I broke the silence by asking if they had lived here long and if they came from the provinces or from abroad. No, they were from around Paris. They'd been living here for two months. That was all she had told me that night. And her first name: Jacqueline.

Van Bever had come down and given me my books. He had asked if I would try to sell them again the next day, and if I made much money this way. They had suggested we meet again. It was difficult for them to give me a precise time, but they could often be found in a café on the corner of the Rue Dante.

I go back there sometimes in my dreams. The other night, a February sunset blinded me as I walked up the Rue Dante. After all these years, it hadn't changed.

I stood at the glassed-in terrace and looked in at the bar, the pinball machine, and the handful of tables, set up as if around a dance floor.

As I crossed the street, the tall apartment building opposite on the Boulevard Saint-Germain cast its shadow over me. But behind me the sidewalk was still lit by the sun.

When I awoke, the time in my life when I had known Jacqueline appeared to me with the same contrast of shadow and light. Pale wintertime streets, and the sun filtering through the slats of the shutters.

Gérard Van Bever wore a herringbone overcoat that was too large for him. I can see him standing at the pinball machine in the café on the Rue Dante. But Jacqueline is the one playing. Her arms and shoulders scarcely move as the machine rattles and flashes. Van Bever's overcoat was voluminous and came down past his knees. He stood very straight, with his collar turned up and his hands in his pockets. Jacqueline wore a gray cable-knit turtleneck and a brown jacket made of soft leather.

The first time I found them at the Café Dante, Jacqueline turned to me, smiled, and went back to her pinball game. I sat down at a table. Her arms and her upper body looked delicate next to the huge machine, whose jolts and shudders threatened to toss her backward at any moment. She was struggling to stay upright, like someone in danger of falling overboard. She came to join me at the table, and Van Bever took his turn at the machine.

At first I was surprised by how much time they spent playing that game. I often interrupted their match; if I hadn't come, it would have gone on indefinitely.

In the afternoon the café was almost empty, but after six o'clock the customers were shoulder to shoulder at the bar and at the tables. I couldn't immediately make out Van Bever and Jacqueline through the roar of conversations, the rattling of the pinball machine, and all the customers squeezed in together. I caught sight of Van Bever's herringbone overcoat first, and then of Jacqueline. I had already come here several times and not found them, and each time I had waited and waited, sitting at a table. I thought I would never see them again, that they had disappeared into the crowds and the noise. And then one day, in the early afternoon, at the far end of the deserted café, they were there, standing side by side at the pinball machine.

I can scarcely remember any other details of that time of my life. I've almost forgotten my parents' faces. I had stayed on a while longer in their apartment, and then I had given up on my studies and begun selling old books for money.

Not long after meeting Jacqueline and Van Bever, I rented a room in a hotel near theirs, the Hôtel de Lima. I had altered the birth date on my passport to make myself one year older and no longer a minor.

The week before I moved into the Hôtel de Lima I had no place to sleep, so they had left me the key to their room while they were out of town at one of the casinos they often went to.

They had fallen into this habit before we met, at the Enghien casino and two or three others in small resort towns in Normandy. Then they had settled on Dieppe, Forges-les-Eaux, and Bagnolles-de-l'Orne. They always left on Saturday and came back on Monday with the money they had won, which was never more than a thousand francs. Van Bever had come up with a martingale 'around the neutral five,' as he said, but it was only profitable if he limited himself to small bets.

I never went with them to the casinos. I waited for them until Monday, never leaving the neighborhood. And then, after a while, Van Bever began going only to 'Forges' – as he called it – because it was closer than Bagnolles-de-l'Orne, while Jacqueline stayed in Paris.

The smell of ether was always hanging in their room when I spent the night alone there. The blue bottle sat on the shelf above the sink. There were clothes in the closet: a man's jacket, a pair of trousers, a bra, and one of the gray turtleneck sweaters that Jacqueline wore.

I slept badly those nights. I woke up not knowing where I was. It took me a long time to recognize the room. If someone had asked me about Van Bever and Jacqueline, I would have had trouble coming up with answers or justifying my presence here. Would they ever come back? I began to doubt it. The man behind the dark wooden counter at the entrance to the hotel was never concerned to see me heading upstairs to their room or keeping the key with me when I went out. He greeted me with a nod.

On the last night, I had awoken about five o'clock and couldn't get back to sleep. I was probably in Jacqueline's bed, and the clock was ticking so loudly that I wanted to put it away in the closet or hide it under a pillow. But I was afraid of the silence. I had got up and left the hotel. I had walked along the quai to the gates of the Jardin des Plantes and then into the only café open that early, across from the Austerlitz train station.

10

The week before, they had gone off to gamble at the Dieppe casino and returned very early in the morning. It would be the same today. One more hour, two more hours to wait. . . . The commuters were emerging from the Gare d'Austerlitz in greater and greater numbers, drinking a cup of coffee at the bar, then heading for the entry to the métro. It was still dark. I walked along the edge of the Jardin des Plantes again, and then along the fence around the old Halle aux Vins.

I spotted their silhouettes from far away. Van Bever's herringbone overcoat stood out in the darkness. They were sitting on a bench on the other side of the quai, facing the closed display cases of the sidewalk book dealers. They were just back from Dieppe. They had knocked on the door of the room, but no one had answered. And I had left not long before, keeping the key in my pocket.

In the Hôtel de Lima, my window overlooked the Boulevard Saint-Germain and the upper end of the Rue des Bernardins. When I lay on the bed I could see the steeple of a church whose name I have forgotten, framed by the window. And the hours rang throughout the night, after the traffic noise had fallen off. Jacqueline and Van Bever often walked me back to my hotel. We had gone to dinner at a Chinese restaurant. We had gone to a movie.

Those nights, nothing distinguished us from the students on the Boulevard Saint-Michel. Van Bever's slightly worn coat and Jacqueline's leather jacket blended in with the drab backdrop of the Latin Quarter. I wore an old raincoat of

11

dirty beige and carried books under my arm. No, there was nothing to draw attention to us.

On the registration form at the Hôtel de Lima I had put myself down as a 'university student,' but this was only a formality, since the man behind the desk had never asked me for any further information. All he asked was that I pay for the room every week. One day as I was leaving with a load of books I was planning to sell to a book dealer I knew, he asked me:

'So, how are your studies going?'

At first I thought I heard something sarcastic in his voice. But he was completely serious.

The Hôtel de la Tournelle was as quiet as the Lima. Van Bever and Jacqueline were the only lodgers. They had explained to me that the hotel was about to close so that it could be converted into apartments. During the day you could hear hammering in the surrounding rooms.

Had they filled out a registration form, and what was their occupation? Van Bever answered that in his papers he was listed as a 'door-to-door salesman,' but he might have been joking. Jacqueline shrugged. She had no occupation. Salesman: I could have claimed the same title, since I spent my days carrying books from one secondhand dealer to the next.

It was cold. The snow melting on the sidewalks and quais, the black and gray of winter come to me in my memory. And Jacqueline always went out in her leather jacket, far too light for that weather.

It was on one of those winter days that Van Bever first went to Forges-les-Eaux alone, while Jacqueline stayed in Paris. She and I walked with Van Bever across the Seine to the Pont-Marie métro stop, since his train would be leaving from the Gare Saint-Lazare. He told us that he might go on to the Dieppe casino as well, and that he wanted to make more money than usual. His herringbone overcoat disappeared into the entrance of the métro and Jacqueline and I found ourselves together.

I had always seen her with Van Bever and had never had an opportunity for a real conversation with her. Besides, she sometimes went an entire evening without saying a word. Or else she would curtly ask Van Bever to go and get her some cigarettes, as if she were trying to get rid of him. And of me too. But little by little I had grown used to her silences and her sharpness.

As Van Bever walked down the steps into the métro that day, I thought she must be sorry not to be setting off with him as she usually did. We walked along the Quai de l'Hôtel-de-Ville instead of crossing over to the Left Bank. She was quiet. I expected her to say good-bye to me at any moment. But no. She continued to walk beside me.

A mist was floating over the Seine and the quais. Jacqueline must have been freezing in that light leather jacket. We

walked along the Square de l'Archevêché, at the end of the
Ile de la Cité, and she began to cough uncontrollably. Finally she caught her breath. I told her she should have something hot to drink, and we entered the café on the Rue Dante.

The usual late-afternoon rush was on. Two silhouettes were
standing at the pinball machine, but Jacqueline didn't want
to play. I ordered a hot toddy for her and she drank it with
a grimace, as if she were taking poison. I told her, 'You
shouldn't go out in such a light jacket.' Even though I had
known her for some time, I had never spoken to her as a
friend. She always kept a sort of distance between us.
    We were sitting at a table in the back, near the pinball ma-
chine. She leaned toward me and said she hadn't left with Van
Bever because she was feeling out of sorts. She was speaking
in a low voice, and I brought my face close to hers. Our
foreheads were nearly touching. She told me a secret: once
winter was over, she planned to leave Paris. And go where?
    'To Majorca . . .'
    I remembered the letter she had mailed the day we met,
addressed to Majorca.
    'But it would be better if we could leave tomorrow . . .'
    Suddenly she looked very pale. The man sitting next to
us had put his elbow on the edge of our table as if he hadn't
noticed us, and he went on talking to the person across from
him. Jacqueline had retreated to the far end of the bench.
The pinball machine rattled oppressively.
    I too dreamt of leaving Paris when the snow melted
on the sidewalks and I went out in my old slip-ons.
    'Why wait until the end of winter?' I asked her.

She smiled.

'We've got to have some money saved up first.'

She lit a cigarette. She coughed. She smoked too much. And always the same brand, with the slightly stale smell of French blond tobacco.

'We'll never save up enough from selling your books.'

I was happy to hear her say 'we,' as if our futures were linked from now on.

'Gérard will probably bring back a lot of money from Forges-les-Eaux and Dieppe,' I said.

She shrugged.

'We've been using his martingale for six months, but it's never made us much money.'

She didn't seem to have much faith in the 'around the neutral five' martingale.

'Have you known Gérard long?'

'Yes . . . we met in Athis-Mons, outside Paris. . . .'

She was looking silently into my eyes. She was probably trying to tell me there was nothing more to say on this subject.

'So you come from Athis-Mons?'

'Yes.'

I knew the name well, since Athis-Mons was near Ablon, where one of my friends lived. He used to borrow his parents' car and drive me to Orly at night. We would go to the movie theater and one of the bars in the airport. We stayed very late listening to the announcements of arrivals and departures for distant places, and we strolled through the central hall. When he drove me back to Paris we never took the freeway, but instead detoured through Villeneuve-le-Roi,

Athis-Mons, other towns in the southern suburbs. I might have passed by Jacqueline one night back then.

'Have you traveled much?'

It was one of those questions people ask to enliven a dull conversation, and I had spoken it in a falsely casual way.

'Not really traveled,' she said. 'But now, if we could get our hands on a little money. . . .'

She was speaking even more quietly, as if she didn't want anyone else to hear. And it was difficult to make out what she said amid all the noise.

I leaned toward her, and again our foreheads were nearly touching.

'Gérard and I know an American who writes novels. . . . He lives on Majorca. . . . He'll find us a house there. We met him in the English bookstore on the quai.'

I used to go to that bookstore often. It was a maze of little rooms lined with books, where it was easy to be alone. The customers came from far away to visit it. It stayed open very late. I had bought a few novels from the Tauchnitz collection there, which I had then tried to sell. Shelves full of books on the sidewalk in front of the shop, with chairs and even a couch. It was like the terrace of a café. You could see Notre Dame from there. And yet once you crossed the threshold, it felt like Amsterdam or San Francisco.

So the letter she had mailed from the Odéon post office was addressed to the 'American who wrote novels. . . .' What was his name? Maybe I had read one of his books. . . .

'William McGivern . . .'

No, I had never heard of this McGivern. She lit another cigarette. She coughed. She was still as pale as before.

16

'I must have the flu,' she said.

'You should drink another hot toddy.'

'No thanks.'

She looked worried all of a sudden.

'I hope everything goes well for Gérard. . . .'

'Me too . . .'

'I'm always worried when Gérard isn't here. . . .'

She had lingered over the syllables of 'Gérard' with great tenderness. Of course, she was sometimes short with him, but she took his arm in the street, or laid her head on his shoulder when we were sitting at one of the tables in the Café Dante. One afternoon when I had knocked on the door to their room, she had told me to come in, and they were both lying in one of the narrow beds, the one nearest the window.

'I can't do without Gérard. . . .'

The words had come rushing out, as if she were speaking to herself and had forgotten I was there. Suddenly I was in the way. Maybe it was best for her to be alone. And just as I was trying to find an excuse to leave, she turned her gaze on me, an absent gaze at first. Then finally she saw me.

I was the one who broke the silence.

'Is your flu any better?'

'I need some aspirin. Do you know of a pharmacy around here?'

So far, my role consisted of directing them to the nearest post office or pharmacy.

There was one near my hotel on the Boulevard Saint-Germain. She bought some aspirin, but also a bottle of ether. We walked together for a few minutes more, to the corner of the Rue des Bernardins. She stopped at the door to my hotel.

'We could meet for dinner, if you like.'

She squeezed my hand. She smiled at me. I had to stop myself from asking if I could stay with her.

'Come and pick me up at seven o'clock,' she said.

She turned the corner. I couldn't help watching her walk toward the quai, in that leather jacket that was too light for this kind of weather. She had put her hands in her pockets.

I spent the afternoon in my room. The heat was off, and I had stretched out on the bed without removing my coat. Now and then I fell half asleep, or stared at a point on the ceiling thinking about Jacqueline and Gérard Van Bever.

Had she gone back to her hotel? Or was she meeting someone, somewhere in Paris? I remembered an evening when she had left Van Bever and me on our own. He and I had gone to see a movie, the late show, and Van Bever seemed nervous. He had taken me to the movies with him so that the time would pass more quickly. About one o'clock in the morning, we had gone to meet Jacqueline in a café on the Rue Cujas. She hadn't told us how she'd spent the evening. And Van Bever hadn't asked any questions, as if my presence were keeping them from speaking freely. I was in the way that night. They had walked me back to the Hôtel de Lima. They were silent. It was a Friday, the day before they usually left for Dieppe or Forges-les-Eaux. I had asked them what train they would be taking.

'We're staying in Paris tomorrow,' Van Bever had said curtly.

They had left me at the entrance to the hotel. Van Bever had said, 'See you tomorrow,' with no good-bye handshake. Jacqueline had smiled at me, a slightly forced smile. She seemed anxious at the prospect of being left alone with Van Bever, as though she wanted someone else around. And yet as I watched them walk away, Van Bever had taken Jacqueline's arm. What were they saying? Was Jacqueline trying to justify something she had done? Was Van Bever rebuking her? Or was I imagining it all?

Night had long since fallen when I left the hotel. I followed the Rue des Bernardins to the quai. I knocked on her door. She came to let me in. She was wearing one of her gray cable-knit turtlenecks and her black pants, narrow at the ankles. She was barefoot. The bed near the window was unmade, and the curtains were drawn. Someone had removed the shade from the bedside lamp, but the tiny bulb left part of the room in shadow. And still that smell of ether, stronger than usual.

She sat down on the edge of the bed, and I took the room's only chair, against the wall, next to the sink.

I asked if she was feeling better.

'A little better . . .'

She saw me looking at the open bottle of ether in the center of the nightstand. It must have occurred to her that I could smell the odor.

'I take that to stop my cough. . . .'

And she repeated in a defensive tone:

19

'It's true . . . it's very good for coughs.'

And since she realized that I was prepared to believe her, she asked:

'Have you ever tried it?'

'No.'

She handed me a cotton ball she had soaked in the ether. I hesitated to take it for a few seconds, but if it would bring us together . . . I inhaled the fumes from the cotton ball and then from the ether bottle. She did the same after me. A coolness filled my lungs. I was lying next to her. We were pressed together, falling through space. The feeling of coolness grew stronger and stronger as the ticking of the clock stood out more and more clearly against the silence, so clearly that I could hear its echo.

We left the hotel at about six o'clock in the morning and walked to the café on the Rue Cujas, which stayed open all night. That was where we had arranged to meet the week before on their return from Forges-les-Eaux. They had arrived at about seven in the morning, and we had eaten breakfast together. But neither of them looked like they had been up all night, and they were much livelier than usual. Especially Jacqueline. They had won two thousand francs.

This time Van Bever would not be coming back by train, but in the car of someone they had met at the Langrune casino, someone who lived in Paris. As we left the hotel, Jacqueline told me he might already be waiting at the café.

I asked whether she wouldn't rather go and meet him alone, whether my presence was really necessary. But she shrugged and said she wanted me to come along.

20

There was no one but us in the café. The fluorescent light blinded me. It was still dark outside, and I had lost my sense of time. We were sitting side by side in a booth near the plate glass window, and it felt like the beginning of the evening.

Through the glass, I saw a black car stop across from the café. Van Bever got out, wearing his herringbone overcoat. He leaned toward the driver before shutting the door. He looked around the room but didn't see us. He thought we were at the far end of the café. He was squinting because of the fluorescent light. Then he came and sat down across from us.

He didn't seem surprised to find me there, or was he too tired to be suspicious? He immediately ordered a double coffee and croissants.

'I decided to go to Dieppe. . . .'

He had kept his overcoat on and his collar turned up. He leaned over the table with his back curved and shoulders hunched, as he often did when he was sitting. In that position, he reminded me of a jockey. When he stood, on the other hand, he stood very straight, as if he wanted to look taller than he was.

'I won three thousand francs at Dieppe. . . .'

He said it with a slightly defiant air. Maybe he was showing his displeasure at finding me there with Jacqueline. He had taken her hand. He was ignoring me.

'That's good,' said Jacqueline.

She was caressing his hand.

'You could buy a ticket for Majorca,' I said.

Van Bever looked at me, astonished.

21

'I told him about our plan,' Jacqueline said.

'So you know about it? I hope you'll come with us. . . .'

No, he definitely didn't seem angry that I was there. But he still spoke to me with a certain formality. Several times I had tried to talk with him like friends. It never worked. He always answered politely but reservedly.

'I'll come along if you want me to,' I told them.

'But of course we want you to,' said Jacqueline.

She was smiling at me. Now she had put her hand over his. The waiter brought the coffee and croissants.

'I haven't eaten for twenty-four hours,' said Van Bever.

His face was pale under the fluorescent lights, and he had circles under his eyes. He ate several croissants very quickly, one after another.

'That's better. . . . A little while ago, in the car, I fell asleep. . . .'

Jacqueline seemed better. She had stopped coughing. Because of the ether? I wondered if I hadn't dreamt the hours I had spent with her, that feeling of emptiness, of coolness and lightness, the two of us in the narrow bed, lurching as if a whirlwind had come over us, the echo of her voice resounding more clearly than the ticking of the alarm clock. There had been no distance between us then. Now she was as aloof as before. And Gérard Van Bever was there. I would have to wait until he went back to Forges-les-Eaux or Dieppe, and there was no way to be sure she would even stay in Paris with me.

'And you, what did you do while I was gone?'

For a moment, I thought he suspected something. But he had asked the question absentmindedly, as if out of habit.

'Nothing in particular,' said Jacqueline. 'We went to the movies.'

She was looking at me as if she wanted me to join in this lie. She still had her hand over his.

'What movie did you see?'

'*Moonfleet*,' I said.

'Was it good?'

He pulled his hand away from Jacqueline's.

'It was very good.'

He looked at us closely one after the other. Jacqueline returned his gaze.

'You'll have to tell me all about it. . . . But some other time . . . there's no hurry.'

There was a sarcastic tone in his voice and I noticed that Jacqueline was looking slightly apprehensive. She frowned. Finally she said to him:

'Do you want to go back to the hotel?'

She had taken his hand again. She had forgotten I was there.

'Not yet . . . I want another coffee. . . .'

'And then we'll go back to the hotel,' she repeated tenderly.

Suddenly I realized what time it was, and the spell was broken. Everything that had made that night extraordinary faded away. Nothing but a pale, dark-haired girl in a brown leather jacket sitting across from a character in a herringbone overcoat. They were holding hands in a café in the Latin Quarter. They were about to go back to their hotel. And another winter day was beginning, after so many others. I would have to wander through the grayness of the

23

Boulevard Saint-Michel once again, among the crowds of people walking to their schools or universities. They were my age, but they were strangers to me. I scarcely understood the language they spoke. One day, I had told Van Bever that I wanted to move to another neighborhood because I felt uncomfortable among all the students. He had said to me:

'That would be a mistake. With them around, no one notices you.'

Jacqueline had turned away, as if she were bored by this subject and worried that Van Bever would tell me something he shouldn't.

'Why?' I had asked him. 'Are you afraid of being noticed?'

He hadn't answered. But I didn't need an explanation. I was always afraid of being noticed too.

'Well? Shall we go back to the hotel?'

She was still speaking in that tender voice. She was caressing his hand. I remembered what she had said that afternoon, in the Café Dante: 'I can't do without Gérard.' They would walk into their room. Would they inhale from the ether bottle, as we had done the night before? No. A little earlier, as we were leaving the hotel, Jacqueline had taken the bottle from her pocket and had thrown it into a sewer farther along the quai.

'I promised Gérard not to touch that filthy stuff anymore.'

Apparently she felt no such scruples with me. I was disappointed, but also strangely happy that she and I were now in collusion, since she had wanted to share 'that filthy stuff' with me.

I walked them back to the quai. As they entered the hotel,
Van Bever held out his hand.

'See you soon.'

She was looking away.

'We'll see each other later at the Café Dante,' she said.

I watched them climb the stairs. She was holding his arm.
I stood still in the entryway. Then I heard the door of their
room closing.

I walked along the Quai de la Tournelle, under the leaf-
less plane trees, in the mist and the wet cold. I was glad to
be wearing snow boots, but the thought of my badly heated
room and brown wooden bed gnawed at me. Van Bever had
won three thousand francs at Dieppe. How would I ever get
hold of that kind of money? I tried to figure the value of the
few books I had left to sell. Not much. In any case, I thought
that even if I had a great deal of money, it would mean nothing to Jacqueline.

She had said, 'We'll see each other later at the Café Dante.'
She had left it vague. So I would have to spend an afternoon
waiting for them, and then another, like the first time. And
as I waited, a thought would come to me: she didn't want to
see me anymore, because of what had happened between us
last night. I had become a problem for her because of what I
knew.

I walked up the Boulevard Saint-Michel, and I felt as
though I'd been walking these same sidewalks since long
before, a prisoner of this neighborhood for no particular
reason. Except one: I had a false student ID card in my
pocket in case I was stopped, so it was better to stay in a
student neighborhood.

25

When I got to the Hôtel de Lima, I hesitated to go in. But I couldn't spend the whole day outside, surrounded by these people with their leather briefcases and satchels, headed for the lycées, the Sorbonne, the École des Mines. I lay down on the bed. The room was too small for anything else: there were no chairs.

The church steeple was framed by the window, along with the branches of a chestnut tree. I wished that I could see them covered with leaves, but it would be another month before spring came. I don't remember if I ever thought about the future in those days. I imagine I lived in the present, making vague plans to run away, as I do today, and hoping to see them soon, him and Jacqueline, in the Café Dante.

They introduced me to Cartaud later on, at around one in the morning. I had waited for them in vain at the Café Dante that evening, and I didn't have the nerve to stop by their hotel. I had eaten in one of the Chinese restaurants on the Rue du Sommerard. The idea that I might never see Jacqueline again killed my appetite. I tried to reassure myself: they wouldn't move out of the hotel just like that, and even if they did, they would leave their new address for me with the concierge. But what particular reason would they have for leaving me their address? No matter; I would spend my Saturdays and Sundays hanging around the casinos of Dieppe and Forges-les-Eaux until I found them.

I spent a long time in the English bookstore on the quai, near Saint-Julien-le-Pauvre. I bought a book there: *A High Wind in Jamaica*, which I had read in French when I was about fifteen, as *Un cyclone à la Jamaïque*. I walked aimlessly for a while, finally ending up in another bookstore, also open very late, on the Rue Saint-Séverin. Then I came back to my room and tried to read.

I went out again and found myself heading for the café where we had met that morning, on the Rue Cujas. My heart jumped: they were sitting in that same booth, near the window, along with a dark-haired man. Van Bever was on his right. Then I could only see Jacqueline, sitting across

27

from them, alone on the bench, her arms folded. She was there behind the glass, in the yellow light, and I wish I could travel back in time. I would find myself on the sidewalk of the Rue Cujas just where I was before, but as I am today, and it would be simple for me to lead Jacqueline out of that fishbowl and into the open air.

I felt sheepish approaching their table as if I were trying to surprise them. Seeing me, Van Bever made a gesture of greeting. Jacqueline smiled at me, showing no surprise at all. Van Bever introduced me to the other man:

'Pierre Cartaud . . .'

I shook his hand and sat down next to Jacqueline.

'Were you in the neighborhood?' asked Van Bever in the polite tone of voice he would have used for a vague acquaintance.

'Yes . . . Completely by chance . . .'

I was very determined to stay where I was, in the booth. Jacqueline was avoiding my gaze. Was it Cartaud's presence that was making them so distant toward me? I must have interrupted their conversation.

'Would you like a drink?' Cartaud asked me.

He had the deep, resonant voice of someone who was practiced at speaking and influencing people.

'A grenadine.'

He was older than us, about thirty-five. Dark, with regular features. He was wearing a gray suit.

Leaving the hotel, I had stuffed *A High Wind in Jamaica* into the pocket of my raincoat. I found it reassuring always to have with me a novel I liked. I set it on the table as I felt deep in my pocket for a pack of cigarettes, and Cartaud noticed it.

'You read English?'

I told him yes. Since Jacqueline and Van Bever were still silent, he finally said:

'Have you known each other long?'

'We met in the neighborhood,' said Jacqueline.

'Oh yes . . . I see. . . .'

What exactly did he see? He lit a cigarette.

'And do you go to the casinos with them?'

'No.'

Van Bever and Jacqueline were still keeping quiet. What could they find so troubling about my being here?

'So you've never seen them play *boule* for three hours straight. . . .'

He let out a loud laugh.

Jacqueline turned to me.

'We met this gentleman at Langrune,' she told me.

'I spotted them right away,' said Cartaud. 'They had such an odd way of playing. . . .'

'Why odd?' said Van Bever, with feigned naïveté.

'And we might ask just what *you* were up to at Langrune?' said Jacqueline, smiling at him.

Van Bever had struck his customary jockey pose: his back curved, his head between his shoulders. He seemed uncomfortable.

'Do you gamble at the casino?' I asked Cartaud.

'Not really. I find it amusing to go there, for no special reason . . . when things are slack. . . .'

And what was his occupation when things weren't slack?

29

Little by little, Jacqueline and Van Bever relaxed. Had they been worried that I might say something to displease Cartaud, or that in the course of our conversation he would reveal something that they both wanted to keep hidden from me?

'And next week . . . Forges?'

Cartaud was looking at them with amusement.

'No, Dieppe,' said Van Bever.

'I could give you a ride there in my car. It's very fast. . . .'

He turned to Jacqueline and me:

'Yesterday it took us a little over an hour to come back from Dieppe. . . .'

So he was the one who had driven Van Bever back to Paris. I remembered the black car stopped on the Rue Cujas.

'That would be very nice of you,' said Jacqueline. 'It's such a bore taking the train every time.'

She was looking at Cartaud in a strange way, as if she found him impressive and couldn't help feeling somehow attracted to him. Had Van Bever noticed?

'I'd be delighted to help you,' said Cartaud. 'I hope you'll join us. . . .'

He was staring at me with his sardonic look. It was as if he had already made up his mind about me and had settled on an attitude of slight condescension.

'I don't go to casinos in the provinces,' I said curtly.

He blinked. Jacqueline was surprised at my reply as well. Van Bever showed no emotion.

'You're missing out. Really very amusing, casinos in the provinces . . .'

His gaze had hardened. I must have offended him. He

30

wasn't expecting that kind of comeback from such a meek-looking boy. But I wanted to ease the tension. So I said:

'You're right. They're very amusing. . . . Especially Langrune . . .'

Yes, I would have liked to know what he was doing at Langrune when he met Jacqueline and Van Bever. I knew the place, because I had spent an afternoon there with some friends during a trip to Normandy the year before. I had a hard time imagining him there, wearing his gray suit and walking along the row of run-down villas by the sea, in the rain, looking for the casino. I vaguely remembered that the casino was not in Langrune itself but a few hundred meters down the road, at Luc-sur-Mer.

'Are you a student?'

He had come around to that question. At first I wanted to say yes, but such a simple answer would only complicate things, since I would have to go on to tell him what I was studying.

'No. I work for book dealers.'

I hoped that would be enough for him. Had he asked Jacqueline and Van Bever the same question? And what was their answer? Had Van Bever told him he was a door-to-door salesman? I didn't think so.

'I used to be a student, just across the way. . . .'

He was pointing at a small building on the other side of the street. 'That was the French School of Orthopedics. I was there for a year. . . . Then I studied dentistry at a school on the Avenue de Choisy. . . .'

His tone had become confidential. Was this really sincere? Maybe he was hoping to make us forget that he was not our age and no longer a student.

'I chose dental school so that I could find a specific direction to take. I had a tendency to drift, like you. . . .'

In the end, I could think of only one explanation for the fact that this thirty-five-year-old man in his gray suit should be sitting with us at this hour in this Latin Quarter café: he was interested in Jacqueline.

'You want something else to drink? I'll have another whiskey. . . .'

Van Bever and Jacqueline did not show the slightest sign of impatience. As for me, I stayed where I was in the booth, like in those nightmares where you can't stand up because your legs are as heavy as lead. From time to time I turned toward Jacqueline, wanting to ask her to leave this café and walk with me to the Gare de Lyon. We would have taken a night train, and the next morning we would have found ourselves on the Riviera or in Italy.

The car was parked a little farther up the Rue Cujas, where the sidewalk became steps with iron handrails. Jacqueline got into the front seat.

Cartaud asked me for the address of my hotel, and we took the Rue Saint-Jacques to reach the Boulevard Saint-Germain.

'If I understand correctly,' he said, 'you all live in hotels. . . .'

He turned his head toward Van Bever and me. He looked

32

us over again with his sardonic smile, and I had the feeling he saw us as utterly insignificant.

'A very Bohemian life, in other words . . .'

Maybe he was trying to strike a flippant and sympathetic tone. If so, he was doing it awkwardly, as older people do who are intimidated by youth.

'And how long will you go on living in hotels?'

This time he was talking to Jacqueline. She was smoking and dropping the ash out the half-open window.

'Until we can leave Paris,' she said. 'It all depends on our American friend who lives on Majorca.'

A little earlier, I had looked for a book by this McGivern person in the English bookstore on the quai but found nothing. The only proof of his existence was the envelope with the Majorcan address that I had seen in Jacqueline's hand that first day. But I wasn't sure the name on the envelope was 'McGivern.'

'Are you sure you can count on him?' Cartaud asked.

Van Bever, sitting next to me, seemed uncomfortable. Finally Jacqueline said:

'Of course . . . He suggested we come to Majorca.'

She was speaking in a matter-of-fact tone I didn't recognize. I got the impression that she wanted to lord it over Cartaud with this 'American friend' and to let him know that he, Cartaud, wasn't the only one interested in her and Van Bever.

He stopped the car in front of my hotel. So this was my cue to say goodnight, and I was afraid I would never see them again, like those afternoons when I waited for them in the Café Dante. Cartaud wouldn't take them straight back

33

to their hotel, and they would end the evening together somewhere on the Right Bank. Or they might even have one last drink somewhere in this neighborhood. But they wanted to get rid of me first.

Van Bever got out of the car, leaving the door open. I thought I saw Cartaud's hand brush Jacqueline's knee, but it might have been an illusion caused by the semidarkness.

She had said good-bye to me, very quietly. Cartaud had favored me with a noncommittal good-night. I was clearly in the way. Standing on the sidewalk, Van Bever had waited for me to get out of the car. And he had shaken my hand. 'One of these days in the Café Dante, maybe,' he'd said.

At the door of the hotel, I turned around. Van Bever waved at me and got back in the car. The door slammed. Now he was alone in the rear seat.

The car started off in the direction of the Seine. That was also the way to the Austerlitz and Lyon train stations, and I thought to myself that they were going to leave Paris.

Before going upstairs to my room I asked the night clerk for a telephone book, but I wasn't quite sure how to spell 'Cartaud,' and I found listings for Cartau, Cartaud, Cartault, Cartaux, Carteau, Carteaud, Carteaux. None of them was named Pierre.

I couldn't get to sleep, and I regretted not having asked Cartaud some questions. But would he have answered? If he had really gone to dental school, did he have a practice now? I tried to imagine him in a white dentist's smock, receiving patients in his office. Then my thoughts returned to Jacqueline, and Cartaud's hand on her knee. Maybe Van Bever could explain some of this for me. I slept restlessly. In my dream, names written in glowing letters were marching by. Cartau, Cartaud, Cartault, Cartaux, Carteau, Carteaud, Carteaux.

I woke up at about eight o'clock: someone was knocking on the door to my room. It was Jacqueline. I must have had the haggard look of someone who hasn't slept well. She said she would wait for me outside.

It was dark. I saw her from the window. She was sitting on the bench across the boulevard. She had turned up the collar of her leather jacket and buried her hands in her pockets to protect herself from the cold.

We walked together toward the Seine and went into the last café before the Halle aux Vins. How was it that she was sitting there, across from me? The night before, getting out of Cartaud's car, I would never have dreamt this could happen so simply. I could only imagine spending many long afternoons waiting for her in the Café Dante, in vain. She explained that Van Bever had left for Athis-Mons to pick up their birth certificates so that they could get new passports. They had lost the old ones during a trip to Belgium three months earlier.

She showed no sign of the indifference that had troubled me so much the night before, when I found them both with Cartaud. She seemed just as she had been before, in the moments we had spent together. I asked her if she was over her flu.

36

She shrugged. It was even colder than yesterday, and she was still wearing that thin leather jacket.

'You should get a real coat,' I told her.

She looked into my eyes and gave me a slightly mocking smile.

'What do you think of as 'a real coat'?'

I wasn't expecting that question. As if she wanted to reassure me, she said:

'Anyway, winter's nearly over.'

She was waiting for news from Majorca. And she expected to be hearing something any day now. She hoped to leave in the spring. Obviously, I would come with them, if I wanted to. I was relieved to hear her say it.

'And Cartaud? What do you hear from him?'

At the mention of the name Cartaud, she frowned. I had spoken in an ordinary tone of voice, like someone talking about the weather.

'You remember his name?'

'It's an easy name to remember.'

And did he have a profession, this Cartaud? Yes, he worked in the office of a dental surgeon on the Boulevard Haussmann, next door to the Jacquemart-André Museum.

With a nervous gesture, she lit a cigarette.

'He might lend us money. That would be useful for our trip.'

She seemed to be watching my reaction intently.

'Is he rich?' I asked her.

She smiled.

'You were talking about a coat, just now. . . . Well, I'll ask him to give me a fur coat. . . .'

She laid her hand on mine, as I had seen her do with Van Bever in the café on the Rue Cujas, and brought her face close to mine.

'Don't worry,' she said. 'I really don't like fur coats at all.'

In my room, she drew the black curtains. I'd never done so before because the color of the curtains bothered me. Every morning the sunlight woke me up. Now the light was streaming through the gap between the curtains. It was strange to see her jacket and her clothes scattered over the floor. Much later, we fell asleep. Comings and goings in the stairway brought me back to consciousness, but I didn't move. She was still sleeping, her head against my shoulder. I looked at my wristwatch. It was two o'clock in the afternoon.

As she left the room, she told me it would be best not to see each other tonight. Van Bever had probably been back from Athis-Mons for some time, and he was expecting her at their hotel on the Quai de la Tournelle. I didn't want to ask how she would explain her absence.

When I was alone again, I felt as though I were back where I had been the night before: once again there was nothing I could be sure of, and I had no choice but to wait here, or at the Café Dante, or maybe to go by the Rue Cujas around one in the morning. And again, on Saturday, Van Bever would leave for Forges-les-Eaux or Dieppe, and we would walk him to the métro station. And if he let her stay in Paris, it would be exactly like before. And so on until the end of time.

I gathered together three or four art books in my beige canvas carryall and went downstairs.

I asked the man standing behind the front desk if he had a directory of the streets of Paris, and he handed me one that looked brand-new, with a blue cover. I looked up all the numbers on the Boulevard Haussmann until I found the Jacquemart-André Museum at number 158. At 160 there really was a dentist, a Pierre Robbes. I wrote down his telephone number, just in case it might be useful: Wagram 13 18. Then, with my beige carryall in my hand, I walked to the English bookstore by Saint-Julien-le-Pauvre, where I managed to sell one of the books I was carrying, *Italian Villas and Their Gardens*, for 150 francs.

I hesitated for a moment before the building at 160 Boulevard Haussmann, and then I stepped into the entryway. On the wall, a plaque listed the names and floors in large printed letters:

Doctor P. Robbes P. Cartaud
3rd floor

The name Cartaud wasn't written in the same lettering as the others, and it seemed to have been inserted sometime afterward. I decided to try the office on the third floor, but I didn't take the elevator, whose cage and glass double doors shone in the semidarkness. Slowly I climbed the stairs, practicing what I would say to the person who came and opened the door – 'I have an appointment with Dr. Cartaud.' If they showed me in to see him, I would take on the jovial tone of someone paying a spur-of-the-moment call on a friend. With this one small difference: he had only seen me once, and it was possible that he wouldn't recognize me.

On the door there was a gilded plaque with the words:

DENTAL SURGEON

I buzzed once, twice, three times, but no one answered.

40

I left the building. Beyond the Jacquemart-André Museum, a café with a glassed-in terrace. I chose a table with a view of the front door of number 160. I waited for Cartaud to arrive. I wasn't even sure he meant anything to Jacqueline and Van Bever. It was only one of those chance meetings. They might never see Cartaud again in their lives.

I had already drunk several grenadines and it was five o'clock in the afternoon. I was beginning to forget just why I was waiting in this café. I hadn't set foot on the Right Bank for months, and now the Quai de la Tournelle and the Latin Quarter seemed thousands of miles away.

Night was falling. The café, which was deserted when I sat down at my table, was gradually filling up with customers who must have come from the offices in the neighborhood. I could hear the sound of a pinball machine, as in the Café Dante.

A black car pulled up alongside the Jacquemart-André Museum. I watched it absently at first. Then suddenly I felt a jolt: it was Cartaud's. I recognized it because it was an English model, not very common in France. He got out of the car and went around to open the left door for someone: it was Jacqueline. They would be able to see me behind the glass wall of the terrace as they walked toward the building's front door, but I didn't move from my table. I even kept my eyes fixed on them, as if I were trying to attract their attention.

They passed by unaware of my presence. Cartaud pushed open the front door to let Jacqueline go in. He was wearing a navy blue overcoat and Jacqueline her light leather jacket.

I bought a token for the telephone at the bar. The phone

41

booth was in the basement. I dialed Wagram 13 18. Someone answered.

'Is this Pierre Cartaud?'

'Who's calling?'

'Could I speak to Jacqueline?'

A few seconds of silence. I hung up.

I met them, her and Van Bever, the next afternoon at the Café Dante. They were alone at the far end of the room, at the pinball machine. They didn't interrupt their game when I came in. Jacqueline was wearing her black pants, narrow at the ankles, and red lace-up espadrilles. They weren't the kind of shoes to wear in winter.

Van Bever went to get some cigarettes, and Jacqueline and I were left alone, facing each other. I took advantage of the moment to say:

'How's Cartaud? How was everything yesterday on the Boulevard Haussmann?'

She became very pale.

'Why do you ask me that?'

'I saw you go into his building with him.'

I was forcing myself to smile and to speak in a light-hearted voice.

'You were following me?'

Her eyes were wide. When Van Bever came back, she leaned toward me and said quietly:

'This stays between us.'

I thought of the bottle of ether – that filthy stuff, as she called it – that I had shared with her the other night.

'You look worried. . . .'

Van Bever was standing before me and had tapped me on

43

the shoulder, as if he were trying to bring me out of a bad dream. He was holding out a pack of cigarettes.

'You want to try another pinball game?' Jacqueline asked him.

It was as if she were trying to keep him away from me.

'Not right now. It gives me a migraine.'

Me too. I could hear the sound of the pinball machine even when I wasn't at the Café Dante.

I asked Van Bever:

'Have you heard from Cartaud lately?'

Jacqueline frowned, probably as a way of telling me to stay off that subject.

'Why? Are you interested in him?'

His voice sounded sharp. He seemed surprised that I had remembered Cartaud's name.

'Is he a good dentist?' I asked.

I remembered the gray suit and the deep, resonant voice, which were not without a certain distinction.

'I don't know,' said Van Bever.

Jacqueline was pretending not to listen. She was looking away, toward the entrance to the café. Van Bever was smiling a little stiffly.

'He works in Paris half the time,' he said.

'And other than that, where does he work?'

'In the provinces.'

The other night, in the café on the Rue Cujas, there was a sort of awkwardness between them and Cartaud, and, despite the mundane conversation we'd had when I sat down at their table, it had never gone away. And I found that same

44

awkwardness now in Jacqueline's silence and Van Bever's evasive replies.

'The trouble with that one is he's hard to get rid of,' said Jacqueline.

Van Bever seemed relieved that she had taken the initiative to let me in on the secret, as if, from now on, they no longer had anything to hide from me.

'We don't particularly want to see him,' he added. 'He comes chasing after us. . . .'

Yes, that was just what Cartaud had said the other night. They had met him two months before in the Langrune casino. He was alone at the *boule* table, playing halfheartedly, just killing time. He had invited them to dinner in the only restaurant that was still open, a little up the road in Luc-sur-Mer, and had explained to them that he worked as a dentist in the area. In Le Havre.

'And do you think it's true?' I asked.

Van Bever seemed surprised that I would express any doubt about Cartaud's profession. A dentist in Le Havre. I had gone there several times, long ago, to board a boat for England, and I'd walked through the streets near the docks. I tried to remember arriving at the train station and going to the port. Big concrete buildings, all the same, lining avenues that seemed too wide. The gigantic buildings and the esplanades had given me a feeling of emptiness. And now I had to imagine Cartaud in that setting.

'He even gave us his address in Le Havre,' Van Bever said.

I didn't dare ask him in front of Jacqueline if he also knew his other address, in Paris, on the Boulevard Haussmann.

45

She had a bemused look all of a sudden, as if she thought
Van Bever was simplifying things and making them much
less confused than they were: a man you meet in a coastal resort in Normandy and who works as a dentist in Le Havre,
all very banal, really. I remembered that I'd always waited
for boarding time in a café by the docks: La Porte Océane. . . .
Did Cartaud go there? And in Le Havre, did he wear the
same gray suit? Tomorrow I would buy a map of Le Havre,
and when I was alone with Jacqueline she would explain it
all for me.

'We thought we would lose him in Paris, but three weeks
ago we saw him again. . . .'

And Van Bever hunched his back a little more and lowered his head between his shoulders, as if he were about to
jump an obstacle.

'You met him in the street?' I asked.

'Yes,' said Jacqueline. 'I ran into him by chance. He was
waiting for a taxi on the Place du Châtelet. I gave him the
address of our hotel.'

Suddenly she seemed very distressed that we were still
talking about this.

'Now that he's in Paris half the time,' said Van Bever, 'he
wants to see us. We can't say no. . . .'

Yesterday afternoon, Jacqueline got out of the car after
Cartaud had opened the door, and followed him into the
building on the Boulevard Haussmann. I had watched them
both. There was no trace of unhappiness on Jacqueline's
face.

'Are you really obligated to see him?'

'In a way,' said Van Bever.

He smiled at me. He hesitated a moment, then added:

'You could do us a favor. . . . Stay with us, next time he hunts us down. . . .'

'Your being there would make things easier for us,' said Jacqueline. 'You don't mind?'

'No, not at all. It will be a pleasure.'

I would have done anything for her.

That Saturday Van Bever went to Forges-les-Eaux. I was
waiting for them in front of their hotel at about five in the
afternoon, as they had asked. Van Bever came out first.
He suggested we take a quick walk along the Quai de la
Tournelle.

'I'm counting on you to keep an eye on Jacqueline.'

These words took me by surprise. A little embarrassed,
he explained that Cartaud had called the day before to say he
wouldn't be able to give him a ride to Forges-les-Eaux because he had work to do. But Cartaud's apparent thoughtful-
ness and false friendliness were not to be trusted. Cartaud
only wanted to take advantage of his absence, Van Bever's,
to see Jacqueline.

So why didn't he take her with him to Forges-les-Eaux?

He answered that if he did, Cartaud would only come
and find them there, and it would be precisely the same
thing.

Jacqueline came out of the hotel to meet us.

'I suppose you were talking about Cartaud,' she said.

She looked at us intently, one after the other.

'I asked him to stay with you,' said Van Bever.

'That's nice.'

We walked him to the Pont-Marie métro station, as before. They were both quiet. And I no longer felt like asking

questions. I was giving in to my natural indifference. All that really mattered was that I would be alone with Jacqueline. I even had Van Bever's authorization to do so, since he had asked me to serve as her guardian. What more could I ask?

Before he walked down the steps into the métro, he said: 'I'll try to be back tomorrow morning.'

At the bottom of the staircase he stood still for a moment, very straight, in his herringbone overcoat. He stared at Jacqueline.

'If you want to get in touch with me, you have the phone number for the casino at Forges. . . .'

Suddenly he had a weary look on his face.

He pushed open one of the doors, and it swung shut behind him.

We were crossing the Ile Saint-Louis heading for the Left Bank, and Jacqueline had taken my arm.

'When are we going to run into Cartaud?'

My question seemed to annoy her slightly. She didn't answer.

I was expecting her to say good-bye at the door of her hotel. But she led me up to her room.

Night had fallen. She turned on the lamp next to the bed.

I was sitting on the chair near the sink, and she was on the floor, with her back against the edge of the bed and her arms around her knees.

'I have to wait for him to call,' she said.

She was talking about Cartaud. But why was she forced to wait for him to call?

'So you were spying on me yesterday on the Boulevard Haussmann?'

'Yes.'

She lit a cigarette. She began to cough after the first puff. I got up from the chair and sat down on the floor next to her. We leaned back against the edge of the bed.

I took the cigarette from her hands. Smoke didn't agree with her, and I wished she would stop coughing.

'I didn't want to talk about it in front of Gérard. . . . He would have been embarrassed with you there. . . . But I wanted to tell you that he knows all about it. . . .'

She was looking defiantly into my eyes:

'For now, there's nothing I can do. . . . We need him. . . .'

I was about to ask her a question, but she reached over and turned off the lamp. She leaned toward me and I felt the caress of her lips on my neck.

'Wouldn't you like to think about something else now?'

She was right. You never knew what trouble the future might hold.

Around seven o'clock in the evening, someone knocked on the door and said in a gravelly voice: 'You're wanted on the telephone.' Jacqueline got up from the bed, slipped on my raincoat, and left the room without turning on the light, leaving the door ajar.

The telephone hung on the wall in the corridor. I could hear her answering yes or no and repeating several times that 'there was really no need for her to come tonight,' as if the person on the other end didn't understand what she was saying, or as if she wanted to be begged.

She closed the door, then came and sat down on the bed. She looked funny in that raincoat; it was too big for her, and she'd pushed the sleeves up.

'I'm meeting him in half an hour. . . . He's going to come and pick me up. . . . He thinks I'm alone here. . . .'

She drew nearer to me and said, in a lower voice:

'I need you to do me a favor. . . .'

Cartaud was going to take her to dinner with some friends of his. After that, she didn't really know how the evening would end. This was the favor she wanted from me: to leave the hotel before Cartaud arrived. She would give me a key. It belonged to the apartment on the Boulevard Haussmann. I was to go and pick up a suitcase, which I would find in one of the cupboards in the dentist's office, 'the one next to the window.' I would take the suitcase and bring it back here, to this room. All very simple. She would call me at about ten o'clock to let me know where to meet her.

What was in this suitcase? She smiled sheepishly and said, 'Some money.' I wasn't particularly surprised. And how would Cartaud react when he found it missing? Well, he would never suspect that we were the ones who had stolen it. Of course, he had no idea that we had a copy of the key to his apartment. She had had it made without his knowledge at the 'Fastkey' counter in the Gare Saint-Lazare.

I was touched by her use of the word 'we,' because she meant herself and me. All the same, I wanted to know if Van Bever was in on this plan. Yes. But he preferred to let her tell me about it. So I was only to play a minor role in all this, and what they wanted from me was a sort of burglary. To help me overcome my qualms, she went on to say that

51

Cartaud wasn't 'a good person,' and that in any case 'he owed it to her. . . .'

'Is it a heavy suitcase?' I asked her.

'No.'

'Because I don't know if it would be better to take a taxi or the métro.'

She seemed amazed that I wasn't expressing any misgivings.

'It doesn't bother you to do this for me?'

She probably wanted to add that I would be in no danger, but I didn't need encouraging. To tell the truth, ever since my childhood, I had seen my father carrying so many bags – suitcases with false bottoms, leather satchels or overnight bags, even those black briefcases that gave him a false air of respectability. . . . And I never knew just what was in them.

'It will be a pleasure,' I told her.

She smiled. She thanked me, adding that she would never again ask me to do anything like this. I was a little disappointed that Van Bever was involved, but there was nothing else at all that bothered me about it. I was used to suitcases.

Standing in the doorway of her room, she gave me the key and kissed me.

I ran down the stairs and quickly crossed the quai in the direction of the Pont de la Tournelle, hoping not to meet up with Cartaud.

In the métro, it was still rush hour. I felt at ease there, squeezed in with the other travelers. There was no risk of drawing attention to myself.

When I came back with the suitcase, I would definitely take the métro.

I waited to switch to the Miromesnil line in the Havre-Caumartin station. I had plenty of time. Jacqueline wouldn't call me at the hotel before ten o'clock. I let two or three trains go by. Why had she sent me on this mission rather than Van Bever? And had she really told him I would be going after the suitcase? With her, you never knew.

Coming out of the métro I was feeling apprehensive, but that soon faded. There were only a few other pedestrians in the street, and the windows of the buildings were dark: offices whose occupants had just left for the day. When I came to number 160 I looked up. Only the fifth-floor windows were lit.

I crossed the lobby in the dark. The elevator climbed slowly and the yellow light of the ceiling lamp over my head cast the shadow of the grillwork onto the stairway wall. I left the elevator door ajar to give me light as I slipped the key into the lock.

Around the vestibule, the double doors of the rooms were all wide open, and there was a white glow coming from the streetlights on the boulevard. I turned to the left and stepped into the dentist's office. Standing in the middle of the room, the chair with its reclining leather back made a sort of elevated couch where you could stretch out if you liked.

By the light from the street I opened the metal cabinet, the one that stood near the windows. The suitcase was there, on a shelf, a simple tinplate suitcase like the ones soldiers on leave carry.

I took the suitcase and found myself back in the vestibule. Opposite the dentist's office, a waiting room. I flipped the switch. Light fell from a crystal chandelier. Green velvet armchairs. On a coffee table, piles of magazines. I crossed the waiting room and entered a little bedroom with a narrow bed, left unmade. I turned on the bedside lamp.

A pajama top lay on the pillow, crumpled into a ball. Hanging in the closet, two suits, the same color gray and the same cut as the one Cartaud was wearing in the café on the Rue Cujas. And beneath the window, a pair of brown shoes, with shoe trees.

So this was Cartaud's bedroom. In the wicker wastebasket I noticed a pack of Royales, the cigarettes Jacqueline smoked. She must have thrown it away the other night when she was here with him.

Without thinking, I opened the nightstand drawer, in which boxes of sleeping pills and aspirin were piled up next to a stack of business cards bearing the name Pierre Robbes, dental surgeon, 160 Boulevard Haussmann, Wagram 13 18.

The suitcase was locked and I hesitated to force it. It wasn't heavy. It was probably full of banknotes. I went through the pockets of the suits and finally found a black billfold holding an identity card, dated a year earlier, in the name of Pierre Cartaud, born 15 June 1923 in Bordeaux (Gironde), address 160 Boulevard Haussmann, Paris.

So Cartaud had been living here for at least a year. . . . And this was also the address of the person known as Pierre Robbes, dental surgeon. It was too late to question the concierge, and I couldn't very well appear at his door with this tinplate suitcase in my hand.

54

I had sat down on the edge of the bed. I could smell ether, and I felt a sudden pang, as if Jacqueline had just left the room.

On my way out of the building I decided to knock on the glass door of the concierge's office, where a light was on. A dark-haired man, not very tall, opened it a crack and put his head out. He looked at me suspiciously.

'I'd like to see Dr. Robbes,' I told him.

'Dr. Robbes isn't in Paris at the moment.'

'Do you have any idea how I could get in touch with him?'

He seemed more and more suspicious, and his gaze lingered on the tinplate suitcase I was carrying.

'Don't you have his address?'

'I can't give it to you, monsieur. I don't know who you are.'

'I'm a relative of Dr. Robbes. I'm doing my military service, and I have a few days' leave.'

That seemed to reassure him a little.

'Dr. Robbes is at his house in Behoust.'

I couldn't quite make out the name. I asked him to spell it for me: BEHOUST.

'I'm sorry,' I said. 'But I thought Dr. Robbes had moved away. There's another name on the list of tenants.'

And I pointed at it, and Cartaud's name.

'He's a colleague of Dr. Robbes. . . .'

I saw the wariness come back into his face. He said:

'Good-bye, monsieur.'

And he quickly closed the door behind him.

Outside, I decided to walk to the métro stop at the Gare Saint-Lazare. The suitcase really wasn't heavy at all. The boulevard was deserted, the façades of the buildings were dark, and from time to time a car passed by, headed for the Place de l'Étoile. It might have been a mistake to knock on the concierge's door, since he would be able to give my description. I reassured myself with the thought that no one – not Cartaud, not the ghostly Dr. Robbes, not the concierge of number 160 – could touch me. Yes, what I had done – entering a strange apartment and taking a suitcase that didn't belong to me, an act that for someone else could be quite serious – was of no consequence for me.

I didn't want to go back to the Quai de la Tournelle right away. I climbed the stairs in the train station and came out into the huge lobby known as the Salle des Pas Perdus. There were still many people heading toward the platforms of the suburban lines. I sat down on a bench with the suitcase between my legs. Little by little I began to feel as though I too were a traveler or a soldier on leave. The Gare Saint-Lazare offered me an escape route that extended far beyond the suburbs or the province of Normandy, where these trains were headed. Buy a ticket for Le Havre, Cartaud's town. And from Le Havre, disappear anywhere, anywhere in the world, through the Porte Océane . . .

Why did they call this the Salle des Pas Perdus, the room of lost steps? It probably took only a little time here before nothing meant anything anymore, not even your footsteps.

I walked to the buffet restaurant at the far end of the lobby. There were two soldiers sitting on the terrace, each with a suitcase identical to mine. I nearly asked them for the little key to their suitcases so that I could try to open the one I was carrying. But I was afraid that once it was open the bundles of banknotes it contained would be visible to everyone around me, and particularly to one of the plainclothes officers I had heard about: the station police. Those two words made me think of Jacqueline and Van Bever, as if they had dragged me into an affair that would expose me to the menace of the station police for the rest of my life.

I went into the buffet restaurant and decided to sit down at one of the tables near the bay windows overlooking the Rue d'Amsterdam. I wasn't hungry. I ordered a grenadine. I kept the suitcase clasped between my legs. There was a couple at the next table speaking in quiet voices. The man was dark-haired, in his thirties, with pockmarked skin over his cheekbones. He hadn't taken off his overcoat. The woman also had dark hair and was wearing a fur coat. They were finishing their dinner. The woman was smoking Royales, like Jacqueline. Sitting next to them, a fat black briefcase and a leather suitcase of the same color. I wondered if they had just arrived in Paris or if they were about to leave. The woman said in a more audible voice:

'We could just take the next train.'

'When is it?'

'Ten fifteen.'

'OK,' said the man.

They were looking at each other in an odd way. Ten fifteen. That was about when Jacqueline would call me at the hotel on the Quai de la Tournelle.

The man paid the check and they stood up. He picked up

the black briefcase and the suitcase. They passed by my table, but they took no notice of me at all.

The waiter leaned down toward me.

'Have you decided?'

He was pointing at the menu.

'This section is reserved for diners. . . . I can't serve you just a drink. . . .'

'I'm waiting for someone,' I told him.

Through the bay window I suddenly saw the man and the woman, on the sidewalk of the Rue d'Amsterdam. He had taken her arm. They walked into a hotel, just a little down the street.

The waiter came back to my table.

'You'll have to make up your mind, monsieur . . . my shift is ending. . . .'

I looked at my watch. Eight fifteen. I wanted to stay where I was rather than wander around outside in the cold, and I ordered the special. Rush hour was over. They'd all taken their trains to the suburbs.

Down below, on the Rue d'Amsterdam, there was a crowd behind the windows of the last café before the Place de Budapest. The light there was yellower and murkier than in the Café Dante. I used to wonder why all these people came and lost themselves in the area around the Gare Saint-Lazare, until I learned that this was one of the lowest areas of Paris. They slid here down a gentle slope. The couple who had been here a moment ago didn't fight the slope. They had let the time of their train go by, to end up in a room with black curtains like the Hôtel de Lima, but with dirtier wallpaper and sheets rumpled by the people who had

58

been there before them. Lying on the bed, she wouldn't even take off her fur coat.

I finished eating. I put the suitcase on the seat next to me. I picked up my knife and tried to fit the end of it into the lock, but the hole was too small. The lock was attached to the suitcase by bolts, which I could have pulled out if I'd had some pliers. Why bother? I would wait until I was with Jacqueline in the room on the Quai de la Tournelle.

I could also leave town on my own and lose contact with her and Van Bever forever. My only good memories up to now were memories of escape.

I thought of cutting a sheet of paper into little squares. On each of the squares, I would write a name and a place:

Jacqueline
Van Bever
Cartaud
Dr. Robbes
160 Boulevard Haussmann, third floor
Hôtel de la Tournelle, 65 Quai de la Tournelle
Hôtel de Lima, 46 Boulevard Saint-Germain
Le Cujas, 22 Rue Cujas
Café Dante
Forges-les-Eaux, Dieppe, Bagnolles-de-l'Orne, Enghien, Luc-sur-Mer, Langrune
Le Havre
Athis-Mons

I would shuffle the papers like a deck of cards and lay them out on the table. So this was my life? So my whole existence at this moment came down to about twenty un-connected names and addresses that had nothing in common but me? And why these rather than others? What did I have to do with these names and places? I was in one of those dreams where you know you can wake up at any time, whenever things turn threatening. If I liked, I could walk away from this table and it would all come undone; everything would disappear into emptiness. There would be nothing left but a tinplate suitcase and a few scraps of paper on which someone had scrawled names and places that no longer meant anything to anyone.

I crossed the Salle des Pas Perdus again, almost deserted now, and walked toward the platforms. I looked at the big board overhead to find the destination of the 10:15 train the couple that had been sitting next to me would take: LE HAVRE. I began to think that none of these trains went anywhere at all, and that we were condemned to wander from the buffet to the Salle des Pas Perdus and from there to the commercial gallery and the surrounding streets. One more hour to kill. I stopped by a telephone booth near the suburban lines. Should I go back to 160 Boulevard Hauss-mann and leave the suitcase where I'd found it? That way everything would be restored to normal and I would have nothing on my conscience. I looked at the phone book in the booth, because I had forgotten Dr. Robbes's number. It rang again and again. There was no one in the apartment. Should I call this Dr. Robbes in Behoust and make a full confession? And where might Jacqueline and Cartaud be right now? I hung up. I decided to keep the suitcase and bring it back to Jacqueline, since that was the only way to stay in contact with her.

I leafed through the phone book. The streets of Paris passed by before my eyes, along with the addresses of buildings and the names of their occupants. I came across SAINT-LAZARE (Gare), and I was surprised to find that there were names there as well:

Railway Police	Lab 28 42
WAGONS-LITS	Eur 44 46
CAFÉ ROME	Eur 48 30
IIOTEL TERMINUS	Eur 36 80
Porters' Cooperative	Eur 58 77
Gabrielle Debrie, florist, Salle des Pas Perdus	Lab 02 47
Commercial Gallery:	
1. Bernois	Eur 45 66
5. Biddeloo et Dilley Mmes	Eur 42 48
Geo Shoes	Eur 44 63
CINÉAC	Lab 80 74
19. Bourgeois (Renée)	Eur 35 20
25. Stop private mail service	Eur 45 96
25 bis. Nono-Nanette	Eur 42 62
27. Discobolos (The)	Eur 41 43

Was it possible to get in touch with these people? Was Renée Bourgeois still somewhere in the station at this hour? Behind the glass of one of the waiting rooms, I could see only a man in an old brown overcoat, slumped on one of the benches, asleep, with a newspaper sticking out of the pocket of his overcoat. Bernois?

I climbed the central staircase and entered the commercial gallery. All the shops were closed. I could hear the sound of diesel engines coming from the taxi stand in the Cour d'Amsterdam. The commercial gallery was very brightly lit, and I was suddenly afraid I might run into one of the agents of the 'Railway Police,' as they were listed in the phone book. He would ask me to open the suitcase and I would have to run. They would have no trouble catching me, and they would drag me into their office in the station. It was too stupid.

I entered the Cinéac and paid my two francs fifty at the ticket counter. The usherette, a blonde with short hair, wanted to lead me to the front rows with her little flashlight, but I preferred to sit in the back. The newsreel pictures were passing by, and the narrator provided a commentary in a grating voice that was very familiar to me: that same voice, for more than twenty-five years. I had heard it the year before at the Cinéma Bonaparte, which was showing a montage of old newsreels.

I had set the suitcase on the seat to my right. I counted seven separate silhouettes in front of me, seven people alone. The theater was filled with that warm smell of ozone that hits you when you walk over a subway grating. I hardly glanced at the pictures of the week's events. Every fifteen minutes these same pictures would appear on the screen, timeless, like that piercing voice, which sounded to me as if it could have been produced through some sort of prosthesis.

The newsreel went by a third time, and I looked at my watch. Nine thirty. There were only two silhouettes left in front of me. They were probably asleep. The usherette was sitting near the entrance on a little seat that folded out from the wall. I heard the seat clack. The beam from her flashlight swept over the row of seats where I was sitting but on the other side of the aisle. She was showing a young man in uniform to his seat. She turned off her flashlight and they sat down together. I overheard a few words of their conversation. He would be taking the train for Le Havre as well. He would try to be back in Paris in two weeks. He would call to let her know the exact date of his return. They were quite close to me. Only the aisle separated us. They were talking out loud, as if they didn't know I and the two sleeping silhouettes in front of us were here. They stopped talking. They were squeezed together, and they were kissing. The grating voice was still discussing the images on the screen: a parade of striking workers, a foreign statesman's motorcade passing through Paris, bombings . . . I wished that voice would fall silent forever. The thought that it would go on just as it was, commenting on future catastrophes without the slightest hint of compassion, sent a shiver down my spine. Now the usherette was straddling her companion's knees. She was moving rhythmically above him, and the springs were squeaking. And soon her sighs and moans drowned out the commentator's quavering voice.

In the Cour de Rome, I looked through my pockets to see if I had enough money left. Ten francs. I could take a taxi. That would be much faster than the métro: I would have had to change at the Opéra station and carry the suitcase through the corridors.

The driver got out to put the suitcase in the trunk, but I

wanted to keep it with me. We drove down the Avenue de l'Opéra and followed the quais. Paris was deserted that night, like a city I was about to leave forever. Once I was at the Quai de la Tournelle, I was afraid I'd lost the key to the room, but it was in one of my raincoat pockets after all.

I walked past the little reception counter and asked the man who usually sat there until midnight if anyone had called for room 3. He answered no, but it was only ten to ten.

I climbed the stairs without any objection from him. Maybe he couldn't tell the difference between Van Bever and me. Or else he didn't feel like worrying about people's comings and goings anymore, in this hotel that was about to be closed down.

I left the door of the room ajar so that I would be sure to hear him when he called me to the telephone. I put the suitcase flat on the floor and stretched out on Jacqueline's bed. The smell of ether clung stubbornly to the pillow. Had she been taking it again? Would that smell be forever associated in my mind with Jacqueline?

At ten o'clock I began to worry: she would never call, and I would never see her again. I often expected people I had met to disappear at any moment, not to be heard from again. I myself sometimes arranged to meet people and never showed up, and sometimes I even took advantage of the momentary distraction of someone I was walking with in the street to disappear. A porte-cochère on the Place Saint-Michel had often been extremely useful to me. Once you passed through it you could cross a courtyard and come out on the Rue de l'Hirondelle. And in a little black notebook I had made a list of all the apartment buildings with two exits. . . .

I heard the man's voice in the stairway: telephone for room 3. It was ten fifteen and I had already given up on her. She had slipped away from Cartaud. She was in the seventeenth arrondissement. She asked if I had the suitcase. I was to pack her clothes in an overnight bag and go get my things as well from the Hôtel de Lima, then wait for her in the Café Dante. But I had to get away from the Quai de la Tournelle as quickly as possible, because that was the first place Cartaud would come looking. She spoke in a very calm voice, as if she had prepared all this in her head beforehand. I found an old overnight bag in the closet and in it I put her two pairs of pants, her leather jacket, her bras, her pairs of red espadrilles, her turtleneck sweater, and the various toiletries lined up on the shelf above the sink, among them a bottle of ether. There was nothing left but Van Bever's clothes. I left the light on so the concierge would think someone was still in the room, and I closed the door behind me. What time would Van Bever come back? He might very well join us at the Café Dante. Had she called him in Forges or Dieppe, and had she said the same thing to him as she'd said to me?

I left the stairway light off as I went downstairs. I didn't want to attract the concierge's attention carrying this suitcase and overnight bag. He was hunched over a newspaper, doing the crossword puzzle. I couldn't help looking at him as I walked by, but he didn't even lift his head. Out on the Quai de la Tournelle, I was afraid I might hear someone behind me shouting 'Monsieur, monsieur . . . Would you please come back at once. . . .' And I was also expecting to

65

see Cartaud pull alongside me and stop. But once I got to the Rue des Bernardins I calmed down. I quickly went up to my room and put the few clothes and the two books I had left into Jacqueline's bag.

Then I went downstairs and asked for the bill. The night concierge asked me no questions. Outside on the Boulevard Saint-Germain I felt the same euphoria that always welled up in me when I was about to run away.

I sat down at the table in the back of the café and laid the suitcase down flat on the bench. No one sitting at the tables. Only one customer was standing at the bar. On the wall above the cigarettes, the hands of the clock pointed to ten thirty. Next to me, the pinball machine was quiet for the first time. Now I was sure she would come and meet me.

She came in, but she didn't look around for me right away. She went to buy some cigarettes at the counter. She sat down. She spotted the suitcase, then put her elbows on the table and let out a long sigh.

'I managed to get rid of him,' she told me.

They were having dinner in a restaurant near the Place Pereire, she, Cartaud, and another couple. She wanted to get away at the end of the meal, but from the terrace of the restaurant they might have been able to see her walking toward the taxi stand or the métro entrance.

They had left the restaurant, and she had no choice but to get into a car with them. They'd taken her to a nearby bar, in a hotel called Les Marronniers, for one last drink. And in Les Marronniers she had given them the slip. Once she was free, she'd called me from a café on the Boulevard de Courcelles.

She lit a cigarette and began to cough. She lay her hand on mine just as I'd seen her do with Van Bever in the café on

67

the Rue Cujas. And she kept coughing, that terrible cough she had.

I took her cigarette and put it out in the ashtray. She said: 'We both have to leave Paris. . . . Is that all right with you?' Of course it was all right.

'Where would you like to go?' I asked.

'Anywhere.'

The Gare de Lyon was quite close. We only had to walk down the quai to the Jardin des Plantes and cross the Seine. We'd both touched bottom, and now the time had come to give the mud a kick that would bring us to the surface again. Back at Les Marronniers, Cartaud was probably becoming concerned about Jacqueline's absence. Van Bever might still be in Dieppe or Forges.

'What about Gérard? Aren't we going to wait for him?' I asked her.

She shook her head and her features began to crumple up. She was about to dissolve into tears. I realized that the reason she wanted to go away with me was so that she could put an end to an episode of her life. And me too: I was leaving behind me all the gray, uncertain years I had lived up to then.

I wanted to tell her again: 'Maybe we should wait for Gérard.' I said nothing. A silhouette in a herringbone overcoat would remain frozen forever in the winter of that year. A few words would come back to me: the neutral five. And also a brown-haired man in a gray suit, with whom I'd had only the most fleeting encounter, and never learned whether he was a dentist or not. And the faces, dimmer and dimmer, of my parents.

I reached into my raincoat pocket for the key to the apartment on the Boulevard Haussmann that she had given me, and I set it on the table.

'What shall we do with this?'

'We'll keep it as a souvenir.'

No one was left at the bar. I could hear the fluorescent lights crackling in the silence around us. The light they put out contrasted with the black of the terrace windows. It was too bright, like a promise of springs and summers to come.

'We should go south. . . .'

It gave me pleasure to say the word *south*. That night, in that deserted café, under the fluorescent lights, life did not yet have any weight at all, and it was so easy to run. . . . Past midnight. The manager came to our table to tell us that the Café Dante was closing.

In the suitcase we found two thin bundles of banknotes, a pair of gloves, books on dental surgery, and a stapler. Jacqueline seemed disappointed to see how thin the bundles were.

We decided to pass through London before heading south to Majorca. We left the suitcase at the checkroom in the Gare du Nord.

We had to wait more than an hour in the buffet for our train. I bought an envelope and a stamp, and I mailed the claim stub to Cartaud at 160 Boulevard Haussmann. I added a note promising to repay the money in the very near future.

In London that spring only married adults could get a room in a hotel. We ended up in a sort of family boardinghouse in Bloomsbury whose landlady pretended to believe we were brother and sister. She gave us a room that was meant to serve as a smoking room or a library, furnished with three couches and a bookshelf. We could only stay five days, and we had to pay in advance.

After that, by appearing at the front desk one after the other as if we weren't acquainted, we managed to get two rooms in the Cumberland, whose massive façade stood over Marble Arch. But there, too, we left after three days, once they had caught on to the deception.

We really didn't know where we would sleep. After Marble Arch we walked straight ahead, along Hyde Park, and turned onto Sussex Gardens, an avenue that climbed toward Paddington Station. One little hotel followed another along the left-hand sidewalk. We picked one at random, and this time they didn't even ask to see our papers.

Doubt always overtook us at the same time: at night, on the way back to the hotel, as we thought of returning to the room where we were living like fugitives, only as long as the owner allowed us to stay.

We walked up and down Sussex Gardens before we crossed the threshold of the hotel. Neither of us had any desire to go back to Paris. From now on the Quai de la Tournelle and the Latin Quarter were closed to us. Paris is a big city, of course, and we could have moved to another neighborhood where there would be no danger of running into Gérard Van Bever or Cartaud. But it was better not to look back.

How much time went by before we made the acquaintance of Linda, Peter Rachman, and Michael Savoundra? Maybe two weeks. Two endless weeks of rain. We went to the movies as an escape from our room and its mildew-flecked wallpaper. Then we took a walk, always along Oxford Street. We came to Bloomsbury, to the street of the boardinghouse where we had spent our first night in London. And once again we walked the length of Oxford Street, in the opposite direction.

We were trying to put off the moment when we would return to the hotel. We couldn't go on walking in this rain. We could always see another movie or go into a department store or a café. But then we would only have to give up and turn back toward Sussex Gardens.

Late one afternoon, when we had ventured farther along to the other bank of the Thames, I felt myself being overcome by panic. It was rush hour: a stream of suburbanites was crossing Waterloo Bridge in the direction of the station. We were walking across the bridge in the opposite direction, and I was afraid we would be caught up in the oncoming current. But we managed to free ourselves. We sat down on a bench in Trafalgar Square. We hadn't spoken a single word as we walked.

'Is something wrong?' Jacqueline asked me. 'You're so pale. . . .'

She was smiling at me. I could see that she was struggling to keep calm. The thought of walking back to the hotel through the crowds on Oxford Street was too much to bear. I didn't dare ask if she was feeling as anxious as I was. I said:

'Don't you think this city is too big?'

I tried to smile as well. She was looking at me with a frown.

'This city is too big, and we don't know anyone. . . .'

My voice was desperate. I couldn't get another word out.

She had lit a cigarette. She was wearing her light leather jacket and coughing from time to time, as she used to do in Paris. I missed the Quai de la Tournelle, the Boulevard Haussmann, and the Gare Saint-Lazare. 'It was easier in Paris. . . .'

But I had spoken so softly that I wasn't sure she'd heard

me. She was absorbed in her thoughts. She had forgotten I was there. In front of us, a red telephone booth, from which a woman had just emerged.

'It's too bad there's no one we can call. . . ,' I said.

She turned to me and put her hand on my arm. She had overcome the despair she must have been feeling a moment before, as we were walking along the Strand toward Trafalgar Square.

'All we need is some money to get to Majorca. . . .'

She had been fixated on that idea from the moment I met her, when I saw the address on the envelope.

'In Majorca things will be easier for us. You'll be able to write your books. . . .'

One day I had let slip that I hoped to write books someday, but we had never talked about it again. Maybe she mentioned it now as a way of reassuring me. She really was a much steadier person than I was.

All the same, I wondered how she was planning to find the money. She didn't flinch:

'It's only in big cities that you can find money. . . . Imagine if we were stuck in some backwater out in the middle of nowhere . . .'

Yes, she was right. Suddenly Trafalgar Square looked much friendlier to me. I was watching the water flow from the fountains, and that helped calmed me. We were not condemned to stay in this city and drown in the crowds on Oxford Street. We had a very simple goal: to find some money and go to Majorca. It was like Van Bever's martingale. With all the streets and intersections around us our chances only

74

increased, and we would surely bring about a happy coincidence in the end.

From then on we avoided Oxford Street and the center of town, and we always walked west toward Holland Park and the Kensington neighborhood.

One afternoon, at the Holland Park underground station, we had our pictures taken in a Photomat. We posed with our faces close together. I kept the pictures as a souvenir. Jacqueline's face is in the foreground, and mine, slightly set back, is cut off by the edge of the photo so that my left ear can't be seen. After the flash we couldn't stop laughing, and she wanted to stay on my knees in the booth. Then we followed the avenue alongside Holland Park, past the big white houses with their porticoes. The sun was shining for the first time since our arrival in London, and as I remember, the weather was always bright and warm from that day onward, as if summer had come early.

At lunchtime, in a café on Notting Hill Gate, we made the acquaintance of a woman named Linda Jacobsen. She spoke to us first. A dark-haired girl, our age, long hair, high cheekbones and slightly slanted blue eyes.

She asked what region of France we were from. She spoke slowly, as if she were hesitating over every word, so it was easy to have a conversation with her in English. She seemed surprised that we were living in one of those seedy Sussex Gardens hotels. But we explained that we had no other choice because we were both underage.

The next day we found her in the same place again, and she came to sit down at our table. She asked if we would be staying long in London. To my great surprise, Jacqueline told her we planned to stay for several months and even to look for work here.

'But in that case you can't go on living in that hotel. . . .'

Every night we longed to move out because of the smell that hung in the room, a sickly sweet smell that might have come from the drains, from a kitchen, or from the rotting carpet. In the morning we would go for a long walk in Hyde Park to get rid of the smell, which impregnated our clothes. It went away, but during the day it would come back, and I would ask Jacqueline:

'Do you smell it?'

76

It was depressing to think that it would be following us for the rest of our lives.

'The worst thing,' Jacqueline told her in French, 'is the smell in the hotel. . . .'

I had to translate for her as best I could. Finally Linda understood. She asked if we had some money. Of the two small bundles in the suitcase, only one was left.

'Not much,' I said.

She looked at us both in turn. She smiled. I was always amazed when people were kind to us. Much later, I found the Photomat picture from Holland Park at the bottom of a shoebox full of old letters, and I was struck by the innocence of our faces. We inspired trust in people. And we had no real qualities, except the one that youth gives to everyone for a very brief time, like a vague promise that will never be kept.

'I have a friend who might be able to help you,' Linda told us. 'I'll introduce you to him tomorrow.'

They often arranged to meet in this café. She lived nearby, and he, her friend, had an office a little way up the street on Westbourne Grove, the avenue with the two movie theaters Jacqueline and I often went to. We always saw the last showing of the evening, as a way of delaying our return to the hotel, and it scarcely mattered to us that we saw the same films every night.

The next day, about noon, we were with Linda when Peter Rachman came into the café. He sat down at our table without even saying hello. He was smoking a cigar and dropping the ash onto the lapels of his jacket.

I was surprised at his appearance: he seemed old to me, but he was only in his forties. He was of average height, quite fat, round face, bald in front and on top, and he wore tortoise-shell glasses. His childlike hands contrasted with his substantial build.

Linda explained our situation to him, but she spoke too quickly for me to understand. He kept his little creased eyes on Jacqueline. From time to time he puffed nervously on his cigar and blew the smoke into Linda's face.

She stopped talking and he smiled at us, at Jacqueline and me. But his eyes were still cold. He asked me the name of our hotel on Sussex Gardens. I told him: the Radnor. He burst out in a brief laugh.

'Don't pay the bill. . . . I own the place. . . . Tell the concierge I said there would be no charge for you. . . .'

He turned to Jacqueline.

'Is it possible that such a pretty woman could be living in the Radnor?'

He had tried to sound suave and worldly, and it made him burst out laughing.

78

'You're in the hotel business?'

He didn't answer my question. Again he blew the smoke from his cigar into Linda's face. He shrugged his shoulders. 'Don't worry. . . ,' he said in English.

He repeated these words several times, speaking to himself. He got up to make a telephone call. Linda sensed that we were a little confused, and she tried to explain some things for us. This Peter Rachman was in the business of buying and reselling apartment houses. Maybe it was too great a stretch to call them 'apartment houses'; they were only decrepit old tenements, scarcely more than hovels, most of them in this neighborhood, as well as in Bayswater and Notting Hill. She didn't understand his business very well. But despite his brutish appearance, he was – she wanted us to know from the start – really a lovely fellow.

Rachman's Jaguar was parked a few steps down the street. Linda got into the front seat. She turned to us:

'You can come and stay with me while you wait for Peter to find you another place. . . .'

He started up the car and followed along Kensington Gardens. Then he turned onto Sussex Gardens. He stopped in front of the Hotel Radnor.

'Go pack your bags,' he told us. 'And remember, don't pay the bill. . . .'

There was no one at the front desk. I took the key to our room from its hook. For the whole of our stay here, we had kept our clothes in our two bags. I picked them up and we went straight downstairs. Rachman was pacing in front of the hotel, his cigar in his mouth and his hands in the pockets of his jacket.

'Happy to be leaving the Radnor?'

He opened the trunk of the Jaguar and I put in our bags. Before starting up again, he said to Linda:

'I have to go by the Lido for a moment. I'll drive you home afterwards. . . .'

I could still smell the sickly odor of the hotel, and I wondered how many days it would be before it disappeared from our lives forever.

The Lido was a bathing establishment in Hyde Park, on the Serpentine. Rachman bought four tickets at the window.

'It's funny. . . . This place reminds me of the Deligny pool in Paris,' I said to Jacqueline.

But once we were inside, we came to a sort of riverside beach, with a few tables and parasols set up around the edge. Rachman chose a table in the shade. He still had his cigar in his mouth. We all sat down. He mopped his forehead and his neck with a big white handkerchief. He turned to Jacqueline:

'Take a swim, if you like. . . .'

'I don't have a suit,' said Jacqueline.

'We can get hold of one. . . . I'll send someone to find you a suit. . . .'

'Don't bother,' Linda said sharply. 'She doesn't want to swim.'

Rachman lowered his head. He was still mopping his forehead and his neck.

'Would you care for some refreshment?' he offered.

Then, speaking to Linda:

'I'm to meet Savoundra here.'

The name conjured up an exotic silhouette in my imagination, and I was expecting to see a Hindu woman in a sari walk toward our table.

But it was a blond man of about thirty who waved in our direction, then came and clapped Rachman on the shoulder. He introduced himself to Jacqueline and me:

'Michael Savoundra.'

Linda told him we were French.

He took one of the chairs from the next table and sat down beside Rachman.

'Well, what's new?' Rachman asked, staring at him with his cold little eyes.

'I've done some more work on the script. . . . We'll see. . . .'

'Yes . . . as you say, we'll see. . . .'

Rachman had taken a disdainful tone. Savoundra crossed his arms, and his gaze lingered on Jacqueline and me.

'Have you been in London long?' he asked in French.

'Three weeks,' I said.

He seemed very interested in Jacqueline.

'I lived in Paris for a while,' he said in his halting French. 'In the Hôtel de la Louisiane, on the Rue de Seine. . . . I tried to make a film in Paris. . . .'

'Unfortunately, it didn't work out,' said Rachman in his disdainful voice, and I was surprised that he had understood the sentence in French.

There was a moment of silence.

'But I'm sure it will work out this time,' said Linda.
'Right, Peter?'

Rachman shrugged. Embarrassed, Savoundra asked Jacqueline, still in French:

'You live in Paris?'

'Yes,' I answered, before Jacqueline could speak. 'Not very far from the Hôtel de la Louisiane.'

Jacqueline's eyes met mine. She winked. Suddenly I longed to be in front of the Hôtel de la Louisiane, to walk to the Seine and stroll past the stands of the secondhand book dealers until I reached the Quai de la Tournelle. Why did I suddenly miss Paris?

Rachman asked Savoundra a question and he answered with a great flurry of words. Linda joined in the conversation. But I wasn't trying to understand them anymore. And I could see that Jacqueline wasn't paying any attention to what they were saying either. This was the time of day when we often dozed off, because we never slept well at the Hotel Radnor, barely four or five hours a night. And since we went out early in the morning and came back as late as possible at night, we often took a nap on the grass in Hyde Park.

They were still talking. From time to time Jacqueline closed her eyes, and I was afraid that I would fall asleep as well. But we gave each other little kicks under the table when we thought that the other one was about to drift off.

I must have dozed for a few moments. The murmur of their conversation blended in with the laughter and shouts coming from the beach and the sound of people diving into the water. Where were we? By the Marne River or the Lake of Enghien? This place reminded me of another Lido, the one in Chenevières, or of the Sporting in La Varenne. Tonight we would go back to Paris, Jacqueline and I, by the Vincennes train.

Someone was tapping me heavily on the shoulder. It was Rachman.

'Tired?'

Across the table from me, Jacqueline was doing her best to keep her eyes wide open.

'You must not have slept much in that hotel of mine,' said Rachman.

'Where were you?' asked Savoundra in French.

'In a place much less comfortable than the Hôtel de la Louisiane,' I told him.

'It's a good thing I ran into them,' said Linda. 'They're going to come and live with me. . . .'

I wondered why they were showing us such kindness. Savoundra's gaze was still fixed on Jacqueline, but she didn't know it, or pretended not to notice. He bore a strong resemblance to an American actor whose name I couldn't quite recall. Of course. Joseph Cotten.

'You'll see,' said Linda. 'You'll be right at home at my place. . . .'

'In any case,' said Rachman, 'there's no lack of apartments. I can let you use one starting next week. . . .'

Savoundra was examining us curiously. He turned to Jacqueline:

'Are you brother and sister?' he asked in English.

'You're out of luck, Michael,' said Rachman icily. 'They're husband and wife.'

Leaving the Lido, Savoundra shook hands with us.

'I hope to see you again very quickly,' he said in French.

Then he asked Rachman if he'd read his script.

'Not yet. I need time. I scarcely know how to read. . . .'

And he let out his short laugh, his eyes as cold as ever behind his tortoise-shell glasses.

Trying to fill the awkward silence, Savoundra turned to Jacqueline and me:

'I'd be very pleased if you would read the script. Some of the scenes take place in Paris, and you could correct the mistakes in the French.'

'Good idea,' said Rachman. 'Let them read it. . . . That way, they can write up a summary for me. . . .'

Savoundra disappeared down a walkway through Hyde Park, and we found ourselves back in the rear seat of Rachman's Jaguar.

'Is his script any good?' I asked.

'Oh yes . . . I'm sure it must be very good,' said Linda.

'You can take it,' said Rachman. 'It's on the floor.'

There was a beige folder lying beneath the rear seat. I picked it up and set it on my knees.

'He wants me to give him thirty thousand pounds to make his movie,' said Rachman. 'That's a lot for a script I'll never read. . . .'

We were back in the Sussex Gardens neighborhood. I was afraid he would take us back to the hotel, and once again I smelled the sickly odor of the hallway and the room. But he kept on driving, in the direction of Notting Hill. He turned right, toward the avenue with the movie theaters, and he entered a street lined with trees and white houses with porticoes. He stopped in front of one of them.

We got out of the car with Linda. Rachman stayed behind the wheel. I took the two bags from the trunk and Linda opened the iron door. A very steep staircase. Linda walked ahead of us. Two doors on the landing. Linda opened the one on the left. A room with white walls. Its windows overlooked the street. No furniture. A large mattress on the floor. There was a bathroom adjoining.

'You'll be comfortable here,' said Linda.

Through the window, I could see Rachman's black car in a patch of sunlight.

'You're very kind,' I told her.

'No, no . . . It's Peter. . . . It belongs to him. . . . He has loads of apartments. . . .'

She wanted to show us her room. Its entrance was the other door on the landing. Clothes and records were scattered over the bed and the floor. There was an odor here too, as penetrating as the one in the Hotel Radnor, but sweeter: the smell of marijuana.

'Don't look too closely,' Linda said. 'My room is always such a mess. . . .'

Rachman had got out of the car and was standing before the entrance to the house. Once again, he was mopping his neck and forehead with his white handkerchief.

'You probably need some spending money?'

And he held out a light blue envelope. I was about to tell-him we didn't need it, but Jacqueline casually took the envelope from his hand.

'Thanks very much,' she said, as if this were all perfectly natural. 'We'll pay you back as quickly as possible.'

'I hope so,' said Rachman. 'With interest . . . Anyway, I'm sure you'll find some way to express your gratitude. . . .'

He laughed out loud.

Linda handed me a small key ring.

'There are two keys,' she said. 'One for the front door, the other for the apartment.'

They got into the car. And before Rachman drove off, Linda lowered the window on her side:

'I'll give you the address of the apartment, in case you get lost. . . .'

She wrote it on the back of the light blue envelope: 22 Chepstows Villas.

Back in the room, Jacqueline opened the envelope. It held a hundred pounds.

'We shouldn't have taken this money,' I told her.

'Yes we should have. . . . We'll need it to go to Majorca. . . .'

She realized I wasn't convinced.

'We'll need about twenty thousand francs to find a house and to live in Majorca. . . . Once we're there, we won't need anyone anymore. . . .'

She went into the bathroom. I heard water running in the tub.

'This is marvelous,' she called to me. 'It's been so long since I've had a bath. . . .'

I stretched out on the mattress. I was trying hard not to

fall asleep. I could hear the sound of her bathing. At one point, she said to me:

'You'll see how nice it is to have hot water. . . .'

In the sink in our room at the Hotel Radnor we'd only had a thin stream of cold water.

The light blue envelope was sitting next to me on the mattress. A gentle torpor was coming over me, dissolving my scruples.

About seven o'clock in the evening, the sound of Jamaican music coming from Linda's room woke us up. I knocked on her door before we went downstairs. I could smell marijuana.

After a long wait, she opened the door. She was wearing a red terrycloth bathrobe. She stuck her head out.

'I'm sorry. . . . I'm with someone. . . .'

'We just wanted to say good evening,' said Jacqueline.

Linda hesitated, then finally made up her mind to speak:

'Can I ask you to do me a favor? When we see Peter, you mustn't let him find out that I have someone here. . . . He's very jealous. . . . Last time, he came by when I wasn't expecting him, and he was this close to smashing the place up and throwing me out the window.'

'What if he comes tonight?' I said.

'He's away for two days. He went to the seaside, to Blackpool, to buy up some more old dumps.'

'Why is he so kind to us?' Jacqueline asked.

'Peter's very fond of young people. He hardly ever sees anyone his own age. He only likes young people. . . .'

A man's voice was calling her, a very quiet voice, almost drowned out by the music.

'Excuse me. . . . See you soon. . . . And make yourselves at home. . . .'

She smiled and closed the door. The music got louder, and we could still hear it from far away in the street.

'That Rachman seems like an odd type,' I said to Jacqueline.

She shrugged.

'Oh, he's nothing to be afraid of. . . .'

She said it as if she'd already met men of his sort, and found him completely inoffensive.

'At any rate, he likes young people. . . .'

I had spoken those words in a lugubrious tone that made her laugh. Night had fallen. She had taken my arm, and I no longer wanted to ask questions or worry about the future. We walked toward Kensington down quiet little streets that seemed out of place in this huge city. A taxi passed by, and Jacqueline raised her arm to make it stop. She gave the address of an Italian restaurant in the Knightsbridge area, which she had spotted during one of our walks and thought would be a good place to go for dinner when we were rich.

The apartment was quiet, and there was no light under Linda's door. We opened the window. Not a sound from the street. Across the way, under the boughs of the trees, an empty red phone booth was lit up.

That night we felt as though we had lived in this apartment for a long time. I had left Michael Savoundra's script on the floor. I began to read it. Its title was *Blackpool Sun-*

day. The two heroes, a boy and a girl of twenty, wandered through the suburbs of London. They went to the Lido on the Serpentine and to the beach at Blackpool in August. They came from modest families and spoke with a Cockney accent. Then they left England. We next saw them in Paris, and then on an island in the Mediterranean that might have been Majorca, where they were finally living 'the good life.' I summarized the plot for Jacqueline as I went along. According to his introduction, Savoundra hoped to film this script as if it were a documentary, casting a boy and girl who weren't professional actors.

I remembered that he'd suggested I correct the French in the part of the script that took place in Paris. There were a few mistakes, and also some very small errors in the street names of the Saint-Germain-des-Prés neighborhood. As I went further, I thought of certain details that I would add, or others that I would modify. I wanted to tell Savoundra about all this, and maybe, if he was willing, to work with him on *Blackpool Sunday*.

For the next few days I didn't have a chance to see Michael Savoundra again. Reading *Blackpool Sunday* had suddenly given me the desire to write a story. One morning I woke up very early and made as little noise as possible so as not to disturb Jacqueline, who usually slept until noon.

I bought a pad of letter paper in a shop on Notting Hill Gate. Then I walked straight ahead along Holland Park Avenue in the summer morning light. Yes, during our stay in London we were at the very heart of the summer. So I remember Peter Rachman as a huge black silhouette, lit from behind, beside the Serpentine. The strong contrast of shadow and sunlight makes it impossible to distinguish his features. Bursts of laughter. Sounds of diving. And those voices from the beach with their limpid, faraway sound, under the effect of the sun and the hazy heat. Linda's voice. Michael Savoundra's voice asking Jacqueline:

'Have you been in London long?'

I sat down in a cafeteria near Holland Park. I had no idea of the story I wanted to tell. I thought I should put down a few sentences at random. It would be like priming a pump or getting a seized-up engine started.

As I wrote the first words, I realized how much influence *Blackpool Sunday* had on me. But it didn't matter if Savoundra's script served as my springboard. The two heroes arrive at the Gare du Nord one winter evening. They're in Paris for the first time in their lives. They walk through the neighborhood for some time, looking for a place to stay. On the Boulevard de Magenta they find a hotel whose concierge agrees to accept them: the Hôtel d'Angleterre et de Belgique. Next door, at the Hôtel de Londres et d'Anvers, they were turned down because they weren't adults.

They never leave the neighborhood, as if they were afraid to risk wandering any farther. At night, in a café just across from the Gare du Nord, on the corner of the Rue de Compiègne and the Rue de Dunkerque, they are sitting at a table next to a strange couple, the Charells, and it is not quite clear what they are doing here: she is a very elegant-looking blonde, he a dark-haired man with a quiet voice. The couple invites them to an apartment on the Boulevard de Magenta, not far from their hotel. The rooms are half-lit. Mme Charell pours them a drink. . . .

I stopped there. Three and a half pages. The two heroes of *Blackpool Sunday*, on arriving in Paris, immediately find themselves in Saint-Germain-des-Prés, at the Hôtel de la Louisiane. Whereas I prevented them from crossing the Seine, letting them sink in and lose themselves in the depths of the Gare du Nord neighborhood.

The Charells were not in the script. Another liberty I had taken. I was in a hurry to write more, but I was still too inexperienced and lazy to keep my concentration for more than an hour, or to write more than three pages a day.

Every morning I went and wrote near Holland Park, and I was no longer in London but in front of the Gare du Nord and walking along the Boulevard de Magenta. Today, thirty years later, in Paris, I am trying to escape from this month of July 1994 to that other summer, when the breeze gently caressed the boughs of the trees in Holland Park. The contrast of shadow and sun was the strongest I have ever seen.

I had managed to free myself from the influence of *Blackpool Sunday*, but I was grateful to Michael Savoundra for having given me a sort of push. I asked Linda if I could see him. We met one evening, he, Jacqueline, Linda, and I, at the Rio in Notting Hill, a popular bar among Jamaicans. We were the only white people there that evening, but Linda knew the place well. I think this was where she got the marijuana whose smell impregnated the walls of the apartment.

I told Savoundra I'd corrected the French in the section of his script that was set in Saint-Germain-des-Prés. He was worried. He was wondering whether Rachman was going to give him the money, and whether it might not be better to get in touch with some producers in Paris. They were ready to place their faith in 'young people' . . .

'But I hear Rachman likes young people as well,' I observed.

And I looked at Jacqueline, who smiled. Linda repeated pensively:

'It's true. . . . He likes young people. . . .'

A Jamaican in his thirties, small, with the look of a jockey, came to sit next to her. He put his arm around her shoulders. She introduced him to us:

'Edgerose . . .'

All these years I've remembered his name. Edgerose. He said he was pleased to meet us. I recognized the quiet voice of the man who had called to Linda from behind the door to her room.

And as Edgerose was explaining to me that he was a musician and that he'd just come back from a tour of Sweden, Peter Rachman appeared. He walked toward our table, his gaze too unwavering behind his tortoise-shell glasses. Linda made a gesture of surprise.

He came and stood before her, and struck her with the back of his hand.

Edgerose stood up and took hold of Rachman's left cheek between his thumb and index finger. Rachman pulled his head back to get free and lost his tortoise-shell glasses. Savoundra and I tried to separate them. The other Jamaican customers were already gathered around our table. Jacqueline kept her calm. She seemed completely indifferent to this scene. She had lit a cigarette.

Edgerose was holding Rachman by the cheek and pulling him toward the exit, like a teacher expelling a troublesome student from the classroom. Rachman was trying to escape, and with a sudden movement of his left arm he gave Edgerose a punch on the nose. Edgerose let go. Rachman opened the door to the café and stood motionless in the middle of the sidewalk.

I went to join him and held out his tortoise-shell glasses, which I had picked up off the floor. He was suddenly very calm. He rubbed his cheek.

'Thanks, old man,' he said. 'There's no point making a fuss over an English whore. . . .'

He had taken his white handkerchief from the pocket of his jacket and he was carefully wiping the lenses of his glasses. Then he fit them over his eyes with a ceremonious gesture, one hand on each earpiece.

He got into the Jaguar. Before driving away, he lowered the window:

'My one wish for you, old man, is that your fiancée won't turn out to be like all these English whores. . . .'

Sitting around the table, everyone was quiet. Linda and Michael Savoundra seemed uneasy. Edgerose was calmly smoking a cigarette. He had a drop of blood on one of his nostrils.

'Peter's going to be in a hell of a mood,' said Savoundra.

'It'll last a few days,' said Linda with a shrug. 'And then it'll pass.'

Our eyes met, Jacqueline's and mine. I had the feeling we were asking ourselves the same questions: Should we stay on at Chepstows Villas? And what exactly were we doing with these three people? Some Jamaican friends of Edgerose came to say hello to him, and the café was filling up with people and noise. Closing your eyes, you might have thought you were in the Café Dante.

Michael Savoundra insisted on walking us partway home. We had left Linda, Edgerose, and their friends, who had begun to ignore us after a while, as if we were in the way.

Savoundra was walking between Jacqueline and me.

'You must miss Paris,' he said.

'Not really,' said Jacqueline.

'It's different for me,' I told him. 'Every morning, I'm in Paris.'

And I explained that I was working on a novel and that the beginning of it took place in the area of the Gare du Nord.

'My inspiration came from *Blackpool Sunday*,' I admitted to him. 'This is also the story of two young people. . . .'

But he didn't seem to hold it against me. He looked at us both.

'Is it about the two of you?'

'Not exactly,' I said.

He was worried. He was wondering if things would be sorted out with Rachman. Rachman was perfectly capable of giving him a suitcase with the thirty thousand pounds in cash tomorrow morning, without having read the script. Or he might tell him no, blowing a puff of cigar smoke in his face.

According to him, the scene we'd just witnessed was a frequent occurrence. To tell the truth, Rachman found it all very entertaining. It was a way to take his mind off his neurasthenia. His life would have made a good subject for a novel. Rachman had arrived in London just after the war, among other refugees coming from the East. He was born somewhere in the middle of the tangled borders of Austria-

95

Hungary, Poland, and Russia, in one of those little garrison towns that had changed names more than once.

'You should ask him some questions,' Savoundra told me. 'Maybe for you he would be willing to answer. . . .'

We had arrived at Westbourne Grove. Savoundra hailed a passing cab:

'Please forgive me for not walking with you all the way. . . . But I'm dead tired. . . .'

Before disappearing into the taxi, he wrote his address and telephone number on an empty cigarette pack. He was counting on my getting in touch with him as soon as possible so that together we could go over my corrections to *Blackpool Sunday*.

We were alone again, the two of us.

'We could take a walk before we go home,' I said to Jacqueline.

What was awaiting us at Chepstows Villas? Rachman throwing the furniture out the window, as Linda had told us? Or maybe he was staking out the place so that he could catch her, her and her Jamaican friends.

We came upon a little park whose name I've forgotten. It was near the apartment, and I've often looked at a map of London trying to find it. Was it Ladbroke Square, or was it farther along, near Bayswater? The façades of the houses around it were dark, and if the streetlights had been turned off that night we would have been able to find our way by the light of the full moon.

Someone had left the key in the little grillwork gate. I opened it, we entered the park, and I turned the key from the inside. We were locked in here, and no one could ever come in again. A coolness came over us, as if we were following a path through the forest. The leaves on the trees above us were so thick that they scarcely let the moonlight through. The grass hadn't been cut for a long time. We discovered a wooden bench, with gravel spread around it. We sat down. My eyes grew accustomed to the dark and I could make out, in the middle of a square, a stone pedestal on which stood the silhouette of an animal that had been left there, and I wondered if it was a lion or a jaguar, or only a dog.

'It's nice here,' said Jacqueline.

She rested her head on my shoulder. The leaves hid the houses around the park. We no longer felt the stifling heat that for the last few days had been hanging over London, a city where we only had to turn a corner to end up in a forest.

Yes, as Savoundra said, I could have written a novel about Rachman. A sentence that he had jokingly thrown out to Jacqueline, that first day, had worried me:

'I'm sure you'll find some way to express your gratitude. . . .'

He'd said it as she took the envelope with the hundred pounds. One afternoon, I had gone for a walk alone in the Hampstead area because Jacqueline wanted to run some errands with Linda. I came back to the apartment around seven o'clock at night. Jacqueline was alone. An envelope was lying on the bed, the same size and the same light blue color as the first, but this one had three hundred pounds in it. Jacqueline seemed uncomfortable. She had waited for Linda all afternoon, but Linda hadn't shown up. Rachman had come by. He had also waited for Linda. He had given her this envelope, which she'd accepted. And I thought to myself that evening that she had found a way to express her gratitude.

There was a smell of Synthol in the room. Rachman always kept a bottle of that medicine with him. Thanks to Linda, I had learned what his habits were. She'd told me that when he went out to dinner at a restaurant he brought along his own dishes and toured the kitchens before the meal to be sure they were clean. He bathed three times a day, and rubbed his body with Synthol. In cafés he ordered a bottle of mineral water, which he insisted on opening himself, and he drank from the bottle so that his lips would not touch a glass that hadn't been washed properly.

He kept girls much younger than he was, and he put them up in apartments like the one in Chepstows Villas. He came to see them in the afternoon, and, without undressing, with no preliminaries, ordering them to turn their back to him, he took them very quickly, as coldly and mechanically as if he were brushing his teeth. Then he would play a game of chess with them on a little chessboard he always carried with him in his black briefcase.

From then on we were alone in the apartment. Linda had disappeared. We no longer heard Jamaican music and laughter at night. It felt a little strange to us, because we had become accustomed to the ray of light streaming from under Linda's door. I tried several times to call Michael Savoundra, but the phone rang again and again with no answer.

It was as if we had never met them. They had faded into the landscape, and in the end we ourselves could no longer really explain what we were doing in this room. We began to feel as though we'd come here by breaking into the building.

Every morning I wrote one or two pages of my novel and went by the Lido to see if Peter Rachman might be sitting at the same table as the first time, on the beach, beside the Serpentine. No. And the man at the ticket booth, whom I had questioned, didn't know anyone by the name of Peter Rachman. I went by Michael Savoundra's place, on Walton Street. I rang, but there was no answer, and I went into the bakery on the ground floor, whose sign bore the name of a certain Justin de Blancke. Why has that name stayed in my memory? This Justin de Blancke was also unable to tell me anything. He knew Savoundra vaguely, by sight. Yes, a blond man who looked like Joseph Cotten. But he didn't think he was here very often.

Jacqueline and I walked to the Rio, at the far end of Notting Hill, and asked the Jamaican who ran it if he knew anything of Linda and Edgerose. He answered that he hadn't heard from them for a few days, and he and the other customers seemed suspicious of us.

One morning as I was coming out of the house as usual with my pad of letter paper, I recognized Rachman's Jaguar parked at the corner of Chepstows Villas and Ledbury Road.

He put his head out the lowered window.

'How are you, old man? Would you like to go for a drive with me?'

He opened the door for me and I sat down next to him.

'We didn't know what had become of you,' I told him.

I didn't dare mention Linda. Maybe he'd been sitting in his car for hours, lying in wait.

'A lot of work . . . A lot of worries . . . Always the same thing . . .'

He was looking at me with his cold eyes behind his tortoise-shell glasses.

'What about you? Are you happy?'

I answered with an embarrassed smile.

He had stopped the car in a little street full of half-ruined houses, looking as if they had just been through a bombardment.

'You see?' he said. 'This is the sort of place I always work in. . . .'

Standing on the sidewalk, he pulled a ring of keys from a black briefcase he was holding, but he changed his mind and stuffed them into the pocket of his jacket.

'There's no point anymore. . . .'

With one kick he opened the door of one of the houses, a door with peeling paint and nothing but a hole where the lock should have been. We went in. The floor was covered with debris. I was overcome by a smell like the one in the hotel on Sussex Gardens, but stronger. I suddenly felt nauseated. Rachman rummaged through his briefcase again and pulled out a flashlight. He moved the beam of light around him, revealing a rusty old stove at the far end of the room. A steep staircase climbed to the second floor, and its wooden banister was broken.

'Since you have paper and pen,' he said, 'you might take notes. . . .'

He inspected the neighboring houses, which were in the same state of abandonment, and as we went along he dictated information for me to take down, after looking in a little notebook he'd taken from his black briefcase.

The next day I continued my novel on the other side of the sheet where I'd written those notes, and I have kept them to this day. Why did he dictate them to me? Maybe he wanted there to be a copy of them somewhere.

The first place we had stopped, in the Notting Hill neighborhood, was called Powis Square, and it led to Powis Terrace and Powis Gardens. Under Rachman's dictation, I took an inventory of numbers 5, 9, 10, 11, and 12 on Powis Terrace, numbers 3, 4, 6, and 7 on Powis Gardens, and numbers 13, 45, 46, and 47 on Powis Square. Rows of houses with porticoes from the 'Edwardian' era, Rachman told me. They'd been occupied by Jamaicans since the end of the war, but he, Rachman, had bought the lot of them just as they were about to be torn down. And now that no one was living in them anymore, he had come up with the idea of restoring them.

He had found the names of the former occupants, the ones before the Jamaicans. So at number 5 on Powis Gardens, I wrote down one Lewis Jones, and at number 6, a Miss Dudgeon; at number 13 on Powis Square, a Charles Edward Boden, at 46, an Arthur Philip Cohen, at number 47, a Miss Marie Motto. . . . Maybe Rachman needed them now, twenty years later, to sign a paper of some kind, but he really didn't think so. In response to a question I had asked about all these people, he had said that most of them had probably disappeared in the Blitz.

We crossed the Bayswater neighborhood, heading toward Paddington Station. This time we ended up at Orsett Terrace, where the porticoed houses, taller than the last ones, adjoined a railroad track. The locks were still fixed to the front doors, and Rachman had to use his ring of keys. No debris, no mildewed wallpaper, no broken staircases inside, but the rooms showed no trace of human presence, as if these houses were a film set they had forgotten to take down.

'These used to be hotels for travelers,' Rachman told me.

What travelers? I imagined shadows at night, emerging from Paddington Station just as the sirens began to blow.

At the end of Orsett Terrace, I was surprised to see a ruined church that was being demolished. Its nave was already open to the sky.

'I should have bought that as well,' said Rachman.

104

We passed by Holland Park and arrived at Hammersmith. I had never been this far. Rachman stopped on Talgarth Road in front of a row of abandoned houses that looked like cottages or little villas by the seaside. We went into one and climbed to the second floor. The glass in the bow window was broken. You could hear the roar of traffic. In one corner of the room I saw a folding cot, and on it a suit wrapped in cellophane as if it had just come from the cleaners, as well as a pajama top. Rachman noticed that I was looking at it:

'Sometimes I come here for a nap,' he told me.

'Doesn't the sound of the traffic bother you?'

He shrugged. Then he picked up the cellophane-wrapped suit and we went downstairs. He walked ahead of me, the suit folded over his right arm, his black briefcase in his left hand, looking like a traveling salesman leaving the house to set out on a tour of the provinces.

He gently draped the suit over the rear seat of the car and sat down behind the wheel again. He turned the car around, toward Kensington Gardens.

'I've slept in much less comfortable places. . . .'

He looked me over with his cold eyes.

'I was about your age. . . .'

We were following Holland Park Avenue and would soon pass by the cafeteria where I was usually sitting and working on my novel at this time of day. . . .

'At the end of the war, I'd escaped from a camp. . . . I slept in the basement of an apartment building. . . . There were rats everywhere. . . . I thought they'd eat me if I fell asleep. . . .'

He laughed thinly.

'I felt like a rat myself. . . . Besides, for the past four years they'd been trying to convince me that I was a rat. . . .'

We had left the cafeteria behind us. Yes, I could put Rachman into my novel. My two heroes would run into Rachman near the Gare du Nord.

'Were you born in England?' I asked him.

'No. In Lvov, in Poland.'

He had answered curtly, and I knew I would get nothing more out of him.

Now we were driving along Hyde Park, heading toward Marble Arch.

'I'm trying to write a book,' I told him timidly, to get the conversation going again.

'A book?'

Since he was born in Lvov, Poland, before the war, and had survived it, there was no reason why he couldn't be in the Gare du Nord neighborhood now. It was only a matter of chance.

He slowed down by Marylebone Station, and I thought we were going to visit another set of run-down houses by the railroad tracks. But we turned down a narrow street and followed it to Regent's Park.

'A rich neighborhood at last."

He let out a laugh like a whinny.

He had me write down the addresses: 125, 127, and 129 Park Road, at the corner of Lorne Close, three pale green houses with bow windows, the last one half ruined.

After checking the tags attached to the keys on the ring, he opened the door of the middle house. We found ourselves on the second floor, in a room more spacious than the one on Talgarth Road. The glass in the window was intact.

At the end of the room, a folding cot like the one on Talgarth Road. He sat down on it with his black briefcase next to him. Then he mopped his forehead with his white handkerchief.

The wallpaper was coming away in spots and there were floorboards missing.

'You should have a look out the window,' he told me. 'It's worth it.'

It was true. I could see the lawns of Regent's Park and the monumental façades all around. Their white stucco and the green of the lawns gave me a feeling of peace and security.

'Now I'm going to show you something else. . . .'

He stood up. We walked down a hallway with old wires hanging from the ceiling and emerged into a small room at the back of the house. Its window overlooked the railroad tracks leading from Marylebone Station.

'Both sides have their charm,' Rachman said. 'Wouldn't you say, old man?'

Then we went back to the bedroom, on the Regent's Park side.

He sat down on the cot again and opened his black briefcase. He took out two sandwiches wrapped in foil. He offered me one. I sat down on the floor, facing him.

'I think I might leave this house as it is and move in here permanently. . . .'

He bit into his sandwich. I thought of the cellophane-wrapped suit. The one he was wearing now was badly rumpled. There was a button missing from the coat as well, and his shoes were spattered with mud. Despite his maniacal attention to cleanliness and his tireless battle against germs, some days he gave the impression that he was giving up the fight, and that little by little he was going to become a derelict.

He finished gulping down his sandwich. He stretched out on the cot. He reached over and rummaged in his black briefcase, which he'd set on the floor next to the bed. He pulled out a key ring and removed one of the keys.

'Here . . . Take it. . . . And wake me in an hour. You can go for a walk in Regent's Park.'

He rolled onto his side, facing the wall, and let out a long sigh.

'I recommend a visit to the zoo. It's quite close.'

I stood motionless at the window for a moment, in a patch of sunlight, before I noticed that he'd fallen asleep.

One night as Jacqueline and I were coming back to Chep-stows Villas, there was a ray of light shining from under Linda's door. The Jamaican music played once again until very late, and the odor of marijuana invaded the apartment, as it had in our first days here.

Peter Rachman used to throw parties in his bachelor apartment on Dolphin Square, a block of buildings by the Thames, and Linda brought us along. There we saw Michael Savoundra, who had been out of town, meeting with producers in Paris. Pierre Roustang had read the script and found it interesting. Pierre Roustang. Another faceless name floating in my memory, but whose syllables have kept a certain resonance, like all the names you hear when you're twenty years old.

There were many different kinds of people at Rachman's parties. In a few months, a fresh wind would blow over London, with new music and bright clothes. And I believe that on Dolphin Square I met a few of the people who were soon to become important personalities in a city suddenly grown young.

I never wrote in the morning anymore, only from mid-night on. I wasn't trying to take advantage of the tranquillity and silence. I was only putting off the moment when I would have to begin work. And I managed to overcome my laziness every time. I had another reason for choosing that hour to write: I was terrified that the panic I had so often felt those first few days we were in London would come back.

Jacqueline undoubtedly had the same fear, but she needed people and noise around her.

At midnight, she would leave the apartment with Linda. They would go to Rachman's parties or to out-of-the-way spots around Notting Hill. At Rachman's you could meet great numbers of people who would invite you to their parties as well. For the first time in London – said Savoundra – you didn't feel that you were out in the provinces. There was electricity in the air, they said.

I remember our last walks together. I accompanied her to Rachman's house on Dolphin Square. I didn't want to go in and find myself among all those people. The idea of returning to the apartment frightened me a little. I would have to start putting the sentences down on the white page again, but I had no choice.

Those evenings, we'd ask the taxi driver to stop at Victoria Station. And from there we would walk to the Thames through the streets of Pimlico. It was July. The heat was suffocating, but whenever we walked along the iron fences of a park, a breeze washed over us, smelling of privet or linden.

We would say goodnight under the portico. The clusters of apartment buildings on Dolphin Square stood out against the moonlight. The shadows of the trees were cast onto the sidewalk, and the leaves stood motionless. There was not a breath of air. Across the quai, beside the Thames, there was a neon sign advertising a restaurant on a barge,

110

and the doorman stood at the edge of the gangplank. But apparently no one ever went into that restaurant. I used to watch the man standing still for hours in his uniform. There were no more cars driving along the quai at that hour, and I had finally arrived at the tranquil, desolate heart of the summer.

Back in Chepstows Villas I wrote, stretched out on the bed. Then I turned off the light and waited in the dark.

She would come in about three o'clock in the morning, always alone. Linda had disappeared again, sometime before.

She would softly open the door. I pretended to be sleeping.

And then, after a few days, I would stay awake until dawn, but I never again heard her footsteps in the stairway.

Yesterday, Saturday the first of October 1994, I took the métro back to my apartment from the Place d'Italie. I had gone looking for videos in a shop that was supposed to have a better selection than the others. I hadn't seen the Place d'Italie for a long time, and it seemed very different because of the skyscrapers.

I stood near the doors in the métro car. A woman was sitting on the bench in the back of the car, on my left, and I'd noticed her because she was wearing sunglasses, a scarf tied under her chin, and an old beige raincoat. She looked like Jacqueline. The elevated métro followed along the Boulevard Auguste-Blanqui. Her face seemed thinner in the daylight. I could clearly make out the shape of her mouth and her nose. It was her, I gradually became convinced of it.

She didn't see me. Her eyes were hidden behind the sunglasses.

She stood up at the Corvisart station and I followed her onto the platform. She was holding a shopping bag in her left hand and walking wearily, almost staggering, not at all the way she used to. I don't know why, but I'd dreamt of her often lately: I saw her in a little fishing port on the Mediterranean, sitting on the ground, knitting endlessly in the sunlight. Next to her, a saucer where passers-by left coins.

She crossed the Boulevard Auguste-Blanqui and turned

112

onto the Rue Corvisart. I followed her along the street, downhill. She stepped into a grocery store. When she came out, I could tell by the way she was walking that her shopping bag was heavier.

On the little square you come to before the park there was a café with the name Le Muscadet Junior. I watched her through the front window. She was standing at the bar, her shopping bag at her feet, and pouring herself a glass of beer. I didn't want to speak to her, or follow her any farther and learn her address. After all these years, I was afraid she wouldn't remember me.

And today, the first Sunday of fall, I'm in the métro again, on the same line. The train passes above the trees on the Boulevard Saint-Jacques. Their leaves hang over the tracks. I feel as though I'm floating between heaven and earth, and escaping my current life. Nothing holds me to anything now. In a moment, as I walk out of the Corvisart station, with its glass canopy like the ones in provincial train stations, it will be as if I were slipping through a crack in time, and I will disappear once and for all. I will follow the street downhill, and maybe I will happen to run into her. She must live somewhere in this neighborhood.

Fifteen years ago, I remember, I had this same feeling. One August afternoon, I had gone to the town hall of Boulogne-Billancourt to pick up a birth certificate. I had walked back by way of the Porte d'Auteuil and the avenues that run alongside the horse track and the Bois de Boulogne. For the moment, I was living in a hotel room near the quai, just beyond the Trocadéro gardens. I didn't know whether I would stay on permanently in Paris or, to continue the book I had begun on 'seaport poets and novelists,' spend some time in Buenos Aires looking for the Argentine poet Hector Pedro Blomberg. I had been intrigued by a few lines of his verse:

Schneider was killed last night
In the Paraguayan woman's bar
He had blue eyes and a very pale face . . .

A sunny late afternoon. Just before the Porte de la Muette, I'd sat down on a bench in a small park. This neighborhood brought back childhood memories. Bus 63, which I used to catch at Saint-Germain-des-Prés, stopped at the Porte de la Muette, and you had to wait for it about six o'clock at night after spending the day in the Bois de Boulogne. But there was no point in summoning up other more recent memories. They belonged to a previous life I wasn't sure I'd ever lived.

I had taken my birth certificate from my pocket. I was born during the summer of 1945, and one afternoon, about five o'clock, my father had gone to the town hall to sign the papers. I could see his signature on the photocopy they'd given me, an illegible signature. Then he had returned home on foot through the deserted streets of that summer, with the crystalline sound of bicycle bells in the silence. And it was the same season as today, the same sunny late afternoon.

I'd put the birth certificate back in my pocket. I was in a dream, and I had to wake up. The ties connecting me to the present were stretching. It would really have been too bad if I'd ended up on this bench in a sort of amnesia, progressively losing my identity, unable to give my address to

114

passers-by. . . . Fortunately I had that birth certificate in my pocket, like dogs that become lost in Paris but carry their owner's address and phone number on their collar. . . . And I tried to explain to myself why I was feeling so unfixed. I hadn't seen anyone for several weeks. No one I had tried to call was back from vacation yet. And I was wrong to choose a hotel so far from the center of town. At the beginning of the summer I had only planned to stay there a very short time, and then to rent a small apartment or studio. Doubt had crept into my mind: Did I really have any desire to stay in Paris? As long as the summer lasted I would be able to feel as if I were only a tourist, but at the beginning of fall the streets, the people, and the things would revert to their everyday color: gray. And I wasn't sure I still had the courage to fade into that color once again.

It would seem that I had come to the end of a period of my life. It had lasted fifteen years, and now I was going through a slack time before beginning again. I tried to transport myself back fifteen years earlier. Then, too, something had come to an end. I was drifting away from my parents. My father used to meet me in back rooms of cafés, in hotel lobbies, or in train station buffets, as if he were choosing these transitory places to get rid of me and to run away with his secrets. We would sit silently, facing each other. From time to time he would give me a sidelong glance. As for my mother, she spoke to me louder and louder. I could tell by the abrupt way her lips moved, because there was a pane of glass between us, muting her voice.

And then the next fifteen years fell apart: a few blurry faces, a few vague memories, ashes. . . . I felt no sadness about this. On the contrary, I was relieved in a way. I would start again from zero. Of that whole grim succession of days, the only ones that still stood out were from when I knew Jacqueline and Van Bever. Why that episode rather than another? Maybe because it had remained unfinished.

The bench I was sitting on was in the shade now. I crossed the little lawn and sat down in the sun. I felt light. I was responsible to no one, I had no need to mumble excuses or lies. I would become someone else, and my metamorphosis would be so complete that no one I'd met over the past fifteen years would be able to recognize me.

I heard the sound of an engine behind me. Someone was parking a car at the corner of the park and the avenue. The engine shut off. The sound of a car door closing. A woman was walking past the iron fence that surrounded the park. She was wearing a yellow summer dress and sunglasses. She had light brown hair. I hadn't quite made out her face, but I immediately recognized her walk, a lazy walk. She slowed down, as if unsure of which direction to take. And then she seemed to find her way. It was Jacqueline.

I left the park and followed her. I didn't dare catch up with her. Maybe she wouldn't remember me clearly. Her hair was shorter than fifteen years before, but that walk couldn't belong to anyone else.

She went into one of the apartment buildings. It was too late to speak to her. And in any case, what would I have said? This avenue is so far from the Quai de la Tournelle and the Café Dante. . . .

I walked by the entryway to the apartment building and

116

made a note of the number. Was this really where she lived? Or was she paying a call on some friends? I began to wonder if it was possible to recognize people from behind by the way they walk. I turned around and headed back toward the park. Her car was there. I was tempted to leave a note on the windshield with the telephone number of my hotel.

At the garage on the Avenue de New-York, the car I had rented the day before was waiting for me. I had come up with this idea in my hotel room. The neighborhood seemed so empty this August in Paris, and I felt so alone when I went out on foot or in the métro that I found the idea of having a car at my disposal comforting. I would feel as though I could leave Paris at any moment, if I wanted to. For the past fifteen years I'd felt like a captive of others and myself, and all my dreams were the same: dreams of escape, of departing trains that, unfortunately, I always missed. I never made it to the station. I was lost in the corridors of the métro, and when I reached the platform the métro never came. I also dreamt of walking out my door and climbing into a big American car that glided through deserted streets toward the Bois de Boulogne, its engine running silently, and I felt a sensation of lightness and well-being.

The attendant gave me the key, and I saw his surprise when I started out in reverse and nearly ran into one of the gasoline pumps. I was afraid I wouldn't be able to stop at the next red light. That was how it happened in my dreams: the brakes had given out, and I was running all the red lights and driving down one-way streets in the wrong direction.

I managed to park the car in front of the hotel and asked the concierge for a directory. I looked up her address, but there was no Jacqueline at that number. She'd probably got married in the past fifteen years. But whose wife was she?

Delorme (P.)
Dintillac
Jones (E. Cecil)
Lacoste (René)
Walter (J.)
Sanchez-Cirès
Vidal

I only had to call each of these names.

In the phone booth I dialed the first number. It rang for a long time. Then someone answered. A man's voice:

'Yes . . . Hello?'

'Could I speak to Jacqueline?'

'You must be mistaken, monsieur.'

I hung up. I no longer had the nerve to dial the other numbers.

I waited for night to fall before leaving the hotel. I sat down behind the wheel and started the car. I knew Paris well, and I would have taken the most direct route to the Porte de la Muette if I'd been on foot, but in this car I was navigating blind. I hadn't driven for a long time, and I didn't know which streets were one-way. I decided to drive straight ahead.

I went far out of my way along the Quai de Passy and the Avenue de Versailles. Then I turned onto the deserted Boulevard Murat. I could have run the red lights, but it pleased me to obey them. I drove slowly, unhurriedly, like someone cruising along a seaside parkway on a summer night. The stoplights were speaking only to me, with their mysterious and friendly signals.

I stopped in front of the entrance to the apartment building, on the other side of the avenue, under the branches of the first trees in the Bois de Boulogne, where the streetlights created an area of semidarkness. The two swinging doors of the entryway, with their ironwork and glass, were lit up. So were the windows on the top floor. They were open wide, and I could make out a few silhouettes on one of the balconies. I heard music and the murmur of conversation. Several cars came and parked on the street in front of the building, and I was sure that the people getting out of them and stepping into the entryway were all headed for the top floor. At one point, someone leaned over the balcony and called out to two silhouettes walking toward the building. A woman's voice. She was telling the other two the floor number. But it wasn't Jacqueline's voice, or at least I didn't recognize it. I decided not to stay there any longer spying on them, and to go upstairs. If it was Jacqueline's party, I didn't know how she would react to the sight of someone she hadn't heard from in fifteen years walking into her apartment unannounced. We'd only known each other for a short while: three or four months. Not much compared to fifteen years. But surely she hadn't forgotten those days. . . . Unless her present life had erased them, in the same way that the blinding beam from a spotlight throws everything outside its path into the deepest shadows.

I waited for more guests to arrive. This time there were three of them. One of them waved toward the balconies on the top floor. I caught up with them just as they entered the building. Two men and a woman. I said hello. It seemed clear to them that I was also invited upstairs.

We went up in the elevator. The two men spoke with an accent, but the woman was French. They were a little older than me.

I forced myself to smile. I said to the woman:

'It's going to be a very nice time, up there. . . .'

She smiled as well.

'Are you a friend of Darius?' she asked me.

'No. I'm a friend of Jacqueline.'

She seemed not to understand.

'I haven't seen Jacqueline for a long time,' I said. 'Is she well?'

The woman frowned.

'I don't know her.'

Then she exchanged a few words in English with the two others. The elevator stopped.

One of the men rang the doorbell. My hands were sweating. The door opened and from inside I heard a hum of conversation and music. A man with brown, swept-back hair and a dusky complexion was smiling at us. He was wearing a beige suit of heavy cotton.

The woman kissed him on both cheeks.

'Hello, Darius.'

'Hello, my dear.'

He had a deep voice and a slight accent. The two men also greeted him with a 'Hello, Darius.' I shook his hand without speaking, but he didn't seem surprised by my presence.

He led us through the entryway and into a living room with open bay windows. There were guests standing here and there in small groups. Darius and the three people I had come up with in the elevator were heading toward one of the balconies. I followed close behind them. They were stopped by a couple at the edge of the balcony, and a conversation started up.

I stood back. They'd forgotten me. I retreated to the other side of the room and sat down at one end of a couch. At the other end, two young people, pressed together, were speaking quietly to each other. No one was paying any attention to me. I tried to spot Jacqueline among the crowd. About twenty people. I looked at the man they called Darius, over by the threshold of the balcony, a slender silhouette in a beige suit. I thought he must be about forty years old. Could Darius be Jacqueline's husband? The clamor of the conversations was drowned out by music, which seemed to be coming from the balconies.

I examined the face of one woman after another, but in vain; I didn't see Jacqueline. This was the wrong floor. I wasn't even sure she lived in this building. Now Darius was in the middle of the room, a few meters from me, standing with a very elegant blonde woman who was listening to him intently. From time to time she laughed. I tried to make out what language he was speaking, but the music covered his voice. Why not walk up to the man and ask him where Jacqueline was? In his deep, courtly voice he would reveal the solution to this mystery, which was not really a mystery at all: if he knew Jacqueline, if Jacqueline was his wife, or what floor she lived on. It was as simple as that. He was facing in my direction. Now he was listening to the blonde woman and by chance his gaze had come to rest on me. At first, I had the impression that he didn't see me. And then he gave me a friendly little wave with his hand. He seemed surprised that I was sitting alone on the couch, speaking to no one, but I was much more comfortable now than when I came into the apartment, and a memory from fifteen years earlier came back to me. We had arrived in London, Jacqueline and I, at Charing Cross Station, about five o'clock in the afternoon. We had taken a taxi to get to the hotel, which we'd chosen at random from a guidebook. Neither of us knew London. When the taxi turned onto the Mall and that shady, tree-lined avenue opened up before me, the first twenty years of my life fell to dust, like a weight, like handcuffs or a harness that I never thought I would be free of. Just like that, nothing remained of all those years. And if happiness was the fleeting euphoria I felt that afternoon, then for the first time in my existence I was happy.

Later, it was dark, and we were walking aimlessly in the area of Ennismore Gardens. We walked along the iron fence surrounding an abandoned garden. There was laughter, music, and the hum of conversation coming from the top floor of one of the houses. The windows were wide open, and a group of silhouettes stood out against the light. We stayed there, leaning on the garden fence. One of the guests sitting on the edge of the balcony had noticed us and had motioned for us to come up. In big cities, in summertime, people who have long since lost track of each other or who don't even know each other meet one evening on a terrace, then lose each other again. And none of it really matters.

122

Darius had come over to me:

'Have you lost your friends?' he said with a smile.

It took me a moment to understand who he meant: the three people in the elevator.

'They're not really my friends.'

But I immediately wished I hadn't said that. I didn't want him asking himself what I was doing here.

'I haven't known them long,' I told him. 'And they had the idea of bringing me here. . . .'

He smiled again.

'The friends of my friends are my friends.'

But he was uncomfortable because he didn't know who I was. To put him at his ease, I said, as quietly as possible:

'Do you often throw such nice parties?'

'Yes. In August. And always when my wife is away.'

Most of the guests had left the living room. How could they all fit on the balconies?

'I feel so lonely when my wife is away. . . .'

His eyes had taken on a melancholy expression. He was still smiling at me. This was the time to ask him if his wife's name was Jacqueline, but I didn't dare risk it yet.

'And you, do you live in Paris?'

He was probably asking just to be polite. After all, I was his guest, and he didn't want me to be sitting alone on a couch away from all the others.

'Yes, but I don't know if I'm going to stay. . . .'

Suddenly I felt a need to confide in him. It had been three months, more or less, since I had spoken to anyone.

'My work is something I can do anywhere, as long as I have a pen and a sheet of paper. . . .'

123

'You're a writer?'

'If you can call it that. . . .'

He wanted me to tell him titles of my books. Maybe he'd read one.

'I don't think so,' I told him.

'It must be exciting to write, hmm?'

He must not have had much practice with one-to-one conversations on such serious matters.

'I'm keeping you from your guests,' I told him. 'For that matter, I think I might have driven them all away.'

There was almost no one left in the living room or on the balconies.

He laughed lightly:

'Not at all . . . Everyone's gone up to the terrace. . . .'

There were still a few guests left in the living room, ensconced on a couch across the room, a white couch like the one where I was sitting next to Darius.

'It's been a pleasure to make your acquaintance,' he told me.

Then he moved toward the others, among them the blonde woman he had been speaking with a few moments before and the man in the blazer from the elevator.

'Don't you think we need some music here?' he asked them, very loudly, as if he were only there to keep the party going. 'I'll go put on a record.'

He disappeared into the next room. After a moment, the voice of a *chanteuse* came forth.

He sat down with the others on the couch. He had already forgotten me.

It was time for me to leave, but I couldn't tear myself

away from the sound of conversation and laughter coming from the terrace and, from the couch, the voices of Darius and his guests occasionally breaking through the music. I couldn't quite make out what they were saying, and I let myself be lulled by the song.

Someone was ringing the doorbell. Darius stood up and walked toward the front door. He smiled at me as he passed by. The others went on talking, and in the heat of the discussion the man in the blazer was making broad gestures, as if he were trying to convince them of something.

Voices in the entryway. They were coming nearer. I heard Darius and a woman speaking in low tones. I turned around. Darius was standing with a couple, and all three of them were at the threshold of the living room. The man was tall, brown-haired, wearing a gray suit, with rather heavy features, his blue eyes shallow-set. The woman was wearing a yellow summer dress that left her shoulders bare.

'We've come too late,' the man said. 'Everyone has already left. . . .'

He had a slight accent.

'No, no,' said Darius. 'They're waiting for us upstairs.'

He took each of them by the arm.

The woman, whom I had seen in three-quarters profile, turned around. My heart jumped. I recognized Jacqueline. They were walking toward me. I stood up, like a robot.

Darius introduced them to me:

'George and Thérèse Caisley.'

I greeted them with a nod. I looked the so-called Thérèse Caisley squarely in the eyes, but she didn't blink. Apparently she didn't recognize me. Darius seemed embarrassed not to be able to introduce me by name.

'These are my downstairs neighbors,' he told me. 'I'm happy they came. . . . And in any case, they wouldn't have been able to sleep because of the noise. . . .'

Caisley shrugged:

'Sleep? . . . But it's still early,' he said. 'The day is only beginning.'

I tried to make eye contact with her. Her gaze was absent. She didn't see me, or else she was deliberately ignoring my presence. Darius led them across the room to the couch where the others were sitting. The man in the blazer stood up to greet Thérèse Caisley. The conversation started up again. Caisley was very talkative. She hung back a little, with a sullen or bored look. I wanted to walk toward her, take her aside, and quietly say to her:

'Hello, Jacqueline.'

But I stood there petrified, trying to find some common thread connecting the Café Dante or the Hôtel de la Tournelle fifteen years ago to this living room with its bay windows open onto the Bois de Boulogne. There was none. I'd fallen prey to a mirage. And yet, now that I thought about it, these places were all in the same city, not so far from each other. I tried to imagine the shortest possible route to the Café Dante: follow the Boulevard Périphérique as far as the Left Bank, enter the city at the Porte d'Orléans, then drive straight ahead toward the Boulevard Saint-Michel. . . . At that hour, in August, it would hardly have taken a quarter of an hour.

The man in the blazer was speaking to her, and she was

126

listening to him indifferently. She'd sat down on one of the arms of the couch and lit a cigarette. I saw her in profile. What had she done to her hair? Fifteen years ago it came down to her waist, and now she wore it a little above the shoulder. And she was smoking, but she wasn't coughing.

'Will you come up with us?' Darius asked me.

He had left the others on the couch and was standing with George and Thérèse Caisley. Thérèse. Why had she changed her name?

I followed them onto one of the balconies.

'You just have to climb the deck ladder,' said Darius.

He pointed to a stairway with concrete steps at the end of the balcony.

'And where are we setting sail for, captain?' asked Caisley, slapping Darius's shoulder familiarly.

We were behind them, side by side, Thérèse Caisley and I. She smiled. But it was a polite smile, the kind used for strangers.

'Have you ever been up here?' she asked me.

'No. Never. This is the first time.'

'The view must be beautiful.'

She had said these words so coldly and impersonally that I wasn't even sure she was speaking to me.

A large terrace. Most of the guests were sitting in beige canvas chairs.

Darius stopped at one of the groups as he passed by. They were sitting in a circle. I was walking behind Caisley and his wife, who seemed to have forgotten I was there. They met another couple at the edge of the terrace. The four

127

of them stood still and began to talk, she and Caisley leaning against the balustrade. Caisley and the two others were
speaking English. From time to time she punctuated the
conversation with a short sentence in French. I came and
rested my elbows on the parapet of the terrace as well. She
was just behind me. The other three were still speaking in
English. The singer's voice drowned out the murmur of the
conversations and I began to whistle the refrain of the song.
She turned around.

'Excuse me,' I said.

'That's all right.'

She smiled at me, the same vacant smile as before. And
since she was silent again, I had no choice but to add:

'Lovely evening . . .'

The discussion between Caisley and the two others was
growing more animated. Caisley had a slightly nasal voice.

'What's especially pleasant,' I told her, 'is the cool breeze
coming from the Bois de Boulogne. . . .'

'Yes.'

She got out a pack of cigarettes, took one, and offered me
the pack:

'Thanks very much. I don't smoke.'

'You're smart. . . .'

She lit a cigarette with a lighter.

'I've tried to quit several times,' she told me, 'but I just
can't do it. . . .'

'Doesn't it make you cough?'

She seemed surprised by my question.

'I stopped smoking,' I told her, 'because it made me
cough.'

128

There was no reaction. She really didn't seem to recognize me.

'It's a shame you can hear the noise of the Périphérique from here,' I said.

'Do you think so? I can't hear it from my apartment. . . . And I live on the fourth floor.'

'Still, the Périphérique is a very useful thing,' I told her. 'It took me no more than ten minutes to drive here from the Quai de la Tournelle tonight.'

But my words had no effect on her. She was still smiling her cold smile.

'Are you a friend of Darius?'

It was the same question the woman had asked me in the elevator.

'No,' I told her. 'I'm a friend of a friend of Darius . . . Jacqueline. . . .'

I avoided making eye contact with her. I was staring at one of the streetlights below us, beneath the trees.

'I don't know her.'

'Do you spend summers in Paris?' I asked.

'My husband and I are leaving for Majorca next week.'

I remembered our first meeting, that winter afternoon on the Place Saint-Michel, and the letter she was carrying, whose envelope said: Majorca.

'Your husband doesn't write detective novels, does he?'

She gave a sudden laugh. It was strange, because Jacqueline had never laughed like that.

'What on earth would make you think he writes detective novels?'

Fifteen years ago, she had told me the name of an American who wrote detective novels and who might be able to help us get to Majorca: McGivern. Later, I had come across a few of his books, and I'd even thought of searching him out and asking him if he knew Jacqueline by any chance, and what had become of her.

'I had him mixed up with someone else who lives in Spain . . . William McGivern. . . .'

For the first time she looked straight into my eyes, and I thought I could see something conspiratorial in her smile.

'What about you?' she asked me. 'Do you live in Paris?'

'For now. I don't know if I'm going to stay. . . .'

Behind us Caisley was still speaking in his nasal voice, and now he was at the center of a very large group.

'I can work anywhere,' I told her. 'I write books.'

Again, her polite smile, her distant voice:

'Oh really? . . . How interesting. . . . I'd very much like to read your books. . . .'

'I'd be afraid they might bore you. . . .'

'Not at all . . . You'll have to bring them to me one day when you come back to Darius's. . . .'

'With pleasure.'

Caisley had let his gaze fall on me. He was probably wondering who I was and why I was talking to his wife. He came to her and put his arm around her shoulders. His shallow blue eyes never left me.

'This gentleman is a friend of Darius and he writes books.'

I should have introduced myself, but I always feel uncomfortable speaking my own name.

'I didn't know Darius had any writer friends.'

130

He smiled at me. He was about ten years older than us. Where could she have met him? In London, maybe. Yes, she had undoubtedly stayed on in London after we lost contact with each other.

'He thought you were a writer as well,' she said.

Caisley was shaken by a loud burst of laughter. Then he stood up straight, just as he was before: his shoulders stiff, his head high.

'Really, that's what you thought? You think I look like a writer?'

I hadn't given the matter any thought. I didn't care what this Caisley person did for a living. No matter how many times I told myself he was her husband, he was indistinguishable from everyone else standing on the terrace. We were lost, she and I, in a crowd of extras on a movie set. She was pretending to know her part, but I wouldn't be able to avoid giving myself away. They would soon notice that I didn't belong here. I still hadn't spoken, and Caisley was looking at me closely. It was essential that I find something to say:

'I had you mixed up with an American writer who lives in Spain . . . William McGivern. . . .'

Now I'd bought myself some time. But it wouldn't be enough. I urgently needed to find other rejoinders, and to speak them in a natural and relaxed tone of voice so as not to attract attention. My head was spinning. I was afraid I was going to be ill. I was sweating. The night seemed stiflingly close, unless it was only the harsh illumination of the spotlights, the loud chatter of the conversations, the laughter.

'Do you know Spain well?' Caisley asked me.

131

She had lit another cigarette, and she was still staring at me with her cold gaze. I was scarcely able to stammer out:

'No. Not at all.'

'We have a house on Majorca. We spend more than three months a year there.'

And the conversation would go on for hours on this terrace. Empty words, hollow sentences, as if she and I had outlived ourselves and could no longer make even the slightest allusion to the past. She was perfectly comfortable in her part. And I didn't blame her: As I went along I too had forgotten nearly everything about my life, and each time whole stretches of it had fallen to dust I'd felt a pleasant sensation of lightness.

'And what's your favorite time of year in Majorca?' I asked Caisley.

I was feeling better now, the air was cooler, the guests around us less noisy, and the singer's voice very sweet.

Caisley shrugged.

'Every season has its charms in Majorca.'

I turned to her:

'And do you feel the same way?'

She smiled as she had a moment before, when I thought I had glimpsed something conspiratorial.

'I feel exactly as my husband does.'

And then a sort of giddiness came over me, and I said to her:

'It's funny. You don't cough when you smoke anymore.'

Caisley hadn't heard me. Someone had slapped him on the back and he had turned around. She frowned.

'No need to take ether for your cough anymore. . . .'

I'd said it lightly, as if only making conversation. She gave me a look of surprise. But she was as poised as ever. As for Caisley, he was talking to the person next to him.

'I didn't understand what you said. . . .'

Now she was looking away, and her gaze had lost its expression. I shook my head briskly, trying to look like someone waking up suddenly.

'Excuse me. . . . I was thinking of the book I'm writing at the moment. . . .'

'A detective novel?' she asked me, politely but distractedly.

'Not exactly.'

It was no use. The surface remained untroubled. Still waters. Or rather a thick sheet of ice, impossible to penetrate after fifteen years.

'Shall we be going?' asked Caisley.

He had his arm around her shoulders. He was a massive figure, and she seemed very small next to him.

'I'm leaving too,' I said.

'We must say good-night to Darius.'

We looked for him without success among the clusters of guests on the terrace. Then we went downstairs to the living room. At the far end of the room, four people were sitting around a table playing cards in silence. Darius was one of them.

'Well,' said Caisley, 'it's obvious that nothing can compete with poker. . . .'

He shook Darius's hand. Darius stood up and kissed her hand. I shook hands with Darius in turn.

'Come back whenever you like,' he told me. 'The door is always open for you.'

On the landing, I waited to take the elevator.

'We'll say good-bye to you here,' said Caisley. 'We live just downstairs.'

'I left my purse in the car this afternoon,' she told him. 'I'll be right back up.'

'Well, good-bye,' said Caisley, with a nonchalant wave of the arm. 'And it was very nice meeting you.'

He went down the stairs. I heard a door shut. The two of us were in the elevator. She lifted her face toward me:

'My car is down the street a little, near the park. . . .'

'I know,' I told her.

She was looking at me, her eyes wide.

'Why? Are you spying on me?'

'I saw you by chance this afternoon, getting out of your car.'

The elevator stopped, the double doors slid open, but she didn't move. She was still looking at me with a slightly surprised expression.

'You haven't changed much,' she told me.

The double doors closed again with a metallic sound. She lowered her head as if she were trying to shield herself from the light of the ceiling lamp in the elevator.

'And me? Do you think I've changed?'

Her voice was not the same as it was a while ago, on the terrace; it was the slightly hoarse, slightly gravelly voice she used to have.

'No . . . Except your hair and your name. . . .'

134

The avenue was silent. You could hear the trees rustling.

'Do you know this neighborhood?' she asked me.

'Yes.'

I was no longer very sure I did. Now that she was walking next to me, I felt as though I had come to this avenue for the first time. But I wasn't dreaming. The car was still there, under the trees. I gestured toward it:

'I rented a car. . . . And I hardly know how to drive. . . .'

'I'm not surprised. . . .'

She had taken my arm. She stopped and gave me a smile:

'Knowing you, you probably get the brake mixed up with the accelerator. . . .'

I also felt as though I knew her well, even if I hadn't seen her for fifteen years and knew nothing of her life. Of all the people I'd met up to now, she was the one who had stayed in my mind the most. As we walked, her arm in mine, I began to convince myself that we had last seen each other the day before.

We came to the park.

'I think it would be better if I drove you home. . . .'

'Fine with me, but your husband will be expecting you. . . .'

The moment I spoke those words I thought to myself that they rang false.

'No . . . He's probably asleep already.'

We were sitting side by side in the car.

'Where do you live?'

'Not far from here. In a hotel near the Quai de Passy.'

She took the Boulevard Suchet in the direction of the Porte Maillot. It was completely the wrong direction.

'If we see each other every fifteen years,' she said, 'you might not recognize me next time.'

What age would we be then? Fifty years old. And that seemed so strange to me that I couldn't help murmuring,

'Fifty . . .'

as a way of giving the number some semblance of reality.

She drove, sitting a little stiffly, her head high, slowing down at the intersections. Everything around us was silent. Except the rustling of the trees.

We entered the Bois de Boulogne. She stopped the car under the trees, near the booth where you board the little train that runs between the Porte Maillot and the Jardin d'Acclimatation. We were in the shadows, beside the path, and ahead of us the lampposts cast a white light on the miniature train station, the deserted platform, the tiny wagons standing still.

She brought her face near mine and brushed my cheek with her hand, as if she wanted to be sure that I was really there, alive, next to her.

'It was strange, just now,' she said, 'when I walked in and saw you in the living room. . . .'

I felt her lips on my neck. I stroked her hair. It wasn't as long as it used to be, but nothing had really changed. Time had stopped. Or rather, it had returned to the hour shown by the hands of the clock in the Café Dante the night we met there just before closing.

The next afternoon I came to pick up the car, which I'd left in front of the Caisleys' building. Just as I was sitting down behind the wheel I saw Darius walking along the avenue in the bright sunlight. He was wearing beige shorts, a red polo shirt, and sunglasses. I waved my arm at him. He didn't seem at all surprised to find me there.

'Hot day, isn't it? . . . Would you like to come up for a drink?'

I turned down the offer on the pretext that I was meeting someone.

'Everyone's abandoning me. . . . The Caisleys left this morning for Majorca. . . . They're smart. . . . It's ridiculous to spend August in Paris. . . .'

Yesterday, she'd told me she wouldn't be leaving until next week. Once again she'd slipped away from me. I was expecting it.

He leaned over the door of the car:

'All the same, drop by some evening. . . . We've got to stick together in August. . . .'

Despite his smile, he seemed vaguely anxious. Something in his voice.

'I'll come,' I told him.

'Promise?'

'I promise.'

I started the car, but I accelerated too fast in reverse. The car hit the trunk of one of the plane trees. Darius spread his arms in a gesture of commiseration.

I set off toward the Porte d'Auteuil. I was planning to return to the hotel by way of the quais along the Seine. The rear fender was probably damaged, and one of the tires was rubbing against it. I went as slowly as possible.

I began to feel a strange sensation, probably because of the deserted sidewalks, the summer haze, and the silence around me. As I drove down the Boulevard Murat, my uneasiness took shape: I had finally discovered the neighborhood where I used to walk with Jacqueline in my dreams. But we'd never really walked together in this area, or else it was in another life. My heart beat faster, like a pendulum near a magnetic field, until I came out onto the Place de la Porte-de-Saint-Cloud. I recognized the fountains in the middle of the square. I was sure that Jacqueline and I usually turned down a street to the right, behind the church, but I couldn't find it this afternoon.

Another fifteen years have gone by, all running together in the fog, and I've heard nothing from Thérèse Caisley. There was no answer at the telephone number she'd given me, as if the Caisleys had never come back from Majorca.

She might have died sometime in the past year. Maybe I would find her one Sunday on the Rue Corvisart.

It's eleven o'clock at night, in August, and the train has slowed down to pass through the first suburban stations. Deserted platforms under the mauve fluorescent lights, where they used to dream of departures for Majorca and martingales around the neutral five.

Brunoy. Montgeron. Athis-Mons. Jacqueline was born somewhere near here.

The rhythmic sounds of the wagons fell silent, and the train stopped for a moment at Villeneuve-Saint-Georges, before the marshaling yard. The façades on the Rue de Paris, alongside the tracks, are dark and shabby. Once there was a succession of cafés, movie theaters, and garages along here. You can still make out their signs. One of them is still lit, like a night-light, for nothing.

CPSIA information can be obtained at www.ICGtesting.com
Printed in the USA
BVOW02s0452300415

398341BV00002B/17/P